Sacrifice

A Reverse Harem Dragon Fantasy

Ava Sinclair

Pandora's Box
Publishing

Contents

Chapter One

LYLA

*B*y water saved. By water cleansed.

Above my head, a pitcher tilts. I brace myself, trying not to shiver as the water – ice cold and precious – hits the top of my head and cascades down my body. The sound of it splashing over my feet echoes off the cavern walls where shadows move like ghostly forms. They are the shadows of women — women I know so well that I can identify them by their shapes. I search out the dark, swaying silhouette of my mother. It is as distinctive as her cry ringing through the cavern, filling me with sadness I try not to show. I know she prayed to the gods for this day not to come.

By water saved. By water purified.

I shudder again as Myrna, our high priestess and my mother's sister, lifts the hammered silver pitcher once more. A second stream of water flows through my long blonde hair, matting it to my back. I lose count of how many times the water sluices down my body, but surely all the dust and ash must be washed away by now. I do not object, however. I stand there, obedient, until the slow drip of water falling from my body is the only sound save for my mother's stifled sobs.

I step from the pool and lift my arms as two initiates dab my body dry. My mother has fallen silent. I cannot face her for fear it will only make her cry anew. She had wanted me to become one of the priestesses who so carefully dry my skin. She would have had me remain here, even if it meant seeing me only once a year on the Holy Days. Had I joined the Order, at least I'd be safe.

Where I go now, she cannot protect me.

No one can.

The initiates move back and Aunt Myrna steps forward. She looks exactly like my mother, save for the eyes. Hers are wiser, clear and resigned. That she has accepted my fate without a fight does not mean she won't mourn for me later. I know she will. But she will cry alone. A priestess does not show her emotions.

I avert my gaze from hers so she will not see the fear that is starting to build in my chest.

By Earth sustained. By Earth clothed.

I lift my arms and feel the gown slide over my head. It is heavier than I expected, woven from precious metals forged and spun into pliable thread. I have been assured it will protect me from the flames. The gown falls all the way to my feet, covering me, but clinging in a manner that emphasizes the fullness of my femininity. Were this war, I would call it armor. But if this were war, what could armor do for me against a monster?

Myrna turns. "It is time. We must leave. Say your goodbyes." Her voice is strained as she advises my mother, not just as priestess, but as her sister. "Save the tears, Sela," she says, embracing her gently. "Give Lyla wise counsel, and strength. Do not send her away with the memory of your weeping. Promise me."

"I promise, Myrna."

She quietly departs, the other priestesses and initiates following in silent, single file.

My mother waits until the chamber is empty to look me in the eye. In her fiftieth year, she is still beautiful, although she seems to have aged since being told that her only daughter would go to Altar Rock.

"I thought ..." She stops to draw a ragged breath. "I thought after all I went through to bring you into the world that the gods would let me keep you. I thought..."

"Mother..." I reach up, my hand touching the sculpted face so like my own. Her skin is warm and smooth. I long to rush into her open arms for protection and shelter, but to do so would only make it worse. "If not me, it would have been someone else's daughter," I say.

"It should have been," comes her bitter reply. "It should have been anyone but you." She takes my hand, pressing it fiercely to her lips. Hot tears leak from her closed eyes and run over the tops of my fingers as she breaks her promise not to cry. But I understand, and in a way am grateful for the emotion. If my last memory is of my mother crying, I will face death knowing I was loved.

"Thank you," I say when she drops my hand. "Thank you for everything. It was a good life, Mother. I never wanted for anything. Ever. I had all that a girl could ask, and more."

"I want to die." She covers her face with her hands.

"No," I grasp her wrists and pull her hands away. "I forbid it." I use same stern tone she's used with me a hundred times. "The gods will only reunite us if you accept their will, remember? So, you will go on, and one day, we will be together again. We will be reunited on the Sunlit Isle, and walk in the shade of olive trees, and pet the beasts that will all be tame."

My mother was supposed to leave me with a happy thought, but I have taken the initiative to leave us both with one, and now there are no more words, other than to tell her that I am ready.

The hand that clutches mine is shaking. My mother leads me to the mouth of the cavern, and from there the priestesses surround me for the long walk up to the flat rock jutting out over the valley below.

Here, the surface has been swept clear of the ever-present ash left from the burnings. The priestesses have been careful to cleanse the path leading up the mountain, as they've always done when our terrible masters demand a sacrifice. Women like me, who make this journey in the protective circle of priestesses, are to arrive unblemished, bearing no evidence of the world we are leaving. Ironically, we are to be free of the ash the burning creates.

It feels odd, walking on flat, warm stone without fine powder raising small clouds around my feet with each step. The hem of my dress brushes the ground as I move forward, making a clinking noise.

Villagers line the path on either side; to my left and right are familiar faces, the warm smiles now replaced with grim resolution or pity. A few look afraid, but I know their fear is not for me. What they really fear is the possibility that I might take my own life before I meet my pre-ordained fate. It happened before, twelve years ago. A tribute threw herself to her death before she reached the top, denying the masters their due. They punished us all then, for what she did. I still remember huddling with my family and the others in the stone hall. I still remember the horrible force of the wind from above, the whoosh of those mighty wings, and the incredible heat. I remember the women weeping, and the men looking ahead, unable to meet their eyes, impotent in their helplessness to stop what was happening outside. In the morning, we emerged to find half our homes were nothing more than stone hulls, the timbers and thatch roofs burnt to cinders. Most of our crops were destroyed. For the cowardice of that tribute, we would lose a dozen to hunger the following winter.

I will not fail them. It is a mantra I repeat with each step that takes me closer to the top. I look neither right nor left, but fix my eyes on the heavy post up ahead. The priestesses around me fan out into a semicircle as we reach the top. I could do as that girl did twelve years ago, I think. I could rush past them and leap to my death. But instead I stand straight, staring ahead as the rope is tied around my leg. It is long enough that I can walk some ten feet, and I step as close as I can to the edge, taking in the view. The land beyond is a palette of grays and browns. Our rulers keep us contained here by making the valley uninhabitable. Nothing flourishes save for what crops they allow us to grow. All else is kept barren, a constant reminder of their power over us. But even barren, it is beautiful. I stare at the valley, marveling at how the light kisses the mountains beyond with a touch of pink. And I wait.

I do not have to wait long.

It is coming.

At first it just looks to be a speck on the horizon, but even at this distance, I can feel a slight breeze generated by its wings. It is moving fast, getting larger and larger by the second. Behind me, the priestesses resume the chant that started in the stone cavern. It is coming. I can make out its shape. The wind now is so strong it lifts my hair.

By air revealed. By air approaches.

All my life, I've been shielded from this ceremony. All young people are. Even as I stand here, the village children are confined in the hall, protected from seeing what has come for me. We are taught to fear, but rarely glimpse *what* we are told to fear.

We are not allowed to see the dragon. But I see it now.

It's bigger than I could ever imagine. It blocks out the view, blocks out the sun. It is glorious and horrible. I want to hide, but I can't move, can't stop staring at it. I struggle to stand against the wind that has already sent the priestesses fleeing behind a rock. It is coming straight for me, its massive neck stretched flat. Then it drops, straight down, like a stone, out of sight, but I know I am not out of danger. A moment later, the dragon ascends directly in front of me, pumping its huge, leathery wings in an almost leisurely fashion, buoyed by the downdraft it creates. Its massive head, big as a boulder — bigger! — is cocked to one side, and I see its huge eye, the elliptical pupil dark and deep as a chasm, the iris flaming around it like a golden sunburst.

The eye is beautiful. It is wise. It is predatory. It is fixed on me.

The priestesses begin their final chant as the dragon lands on the lip of the ledge, the final draft of its wings forcing me to the ground.

By fire claimed. By fire delivered.

Did the others scream? I look through the curtain of hair that has fallen over my face to see the dragon's head extending towards me. Its nose is inches away; its nostril wider than my arm. It sniffs me, the force of its inhale so strong it pulls me forward. The green scales, each bony plate five times as large as a warrior's shield, flash iridescent in the light.

The head draws back. The dragon stares down at me. I stare back. I will face it. I will not beg. I will not let it take my dignity, even if it takes my life.

The heat is incredible, but the garment protects me. Only the rope is burned by the jet of flame that shoots from its mouth. With the bond keeping me tethered now a line of ash, the huge clawed foot reaches out and closes around me. The dragon lifts me, holds me at eye level, and smiles. And it is this gesture, so human, that finally elicits my scream of terror.

But no one hears it, for the flapping of its wings is louder than my cry as the dragon rises with me in its grasp. It takes me high into the air. The dragon banks to the left, and I look down on the little village, the brownish-grey thread of the river that runs through it, the stone and timber houses, the rows of crops that my sacrifice has spared. The people look like dots. Somewhere down there is my mother, watching from below as her daughter is carried away across the mountains by a dragon.

Chapter Two

DRORGROS

Fear. It is a tool used by the strong to keep the weak in line. Those who would disagree lack the will to do what must be done, even if that means setting the world on fire. Fear is a palpable thing, an instant, primal response in the face of danger. I have sensed it in warriors and kings.

But in her, before fear there was wonder.

Who is this female I have brought to my bed?

She is sleeping. I do not yet know her name. I will find out when she opens her eyes. I will know her name. She will know mine; I will make her scream it.

It is no surprise that she lost consciousness. She is, after all, a mere human. The air is thin so high in the clouds.

She is earthbound now, lying on my bed. I sliced the gown off with my blade, laying her body bare. It is a delectable body, pale and lush, the firm globes of her breasts topped with nipples I know will be sweet as summer berries — sweeter. Her white belly has the hint of a feminine swell. Her legs are well-muscled, shapely. The thatch of golden curls covering the "v" between her thighs is not so thick as to hide the seam of her virgin pussy. The plump lips of her outer labia are closed like hands pressed tight to hide her charms

As the victor, I will be the first to open her. My mighty cock is stiff and eager for what awaits. I could do it now. I could awaken her with one mighty thrust through her virgin barrier. I imagine her eyes flying open in surprise, her full lips forming an "o" of wordless shock. That is how Zelki mused he would do it, before I reminded him I'd won first rights. I'd defeated him, and Tythos and Imryth. Her innocence is mine to claim.

And I can do it as I wish. I could take her as she is, but I prefer the sound of a woman's moans of pleasure to her cries of distress. I will make her beg - not for me to spare her virginity, but to take it.

She stirs on the bed and whimpers, the motion jostling her breasts. My cock hardens almost painfully as I imagine our sons nursing those breasts. I can see it in my mind's eye, sturdy male babes folded in those soft arms, pulling at her long blonde hair with their tiny fists as they suckle her tits. But I shall taste them first.

So small, so vulnerable. And a short time ago, so oblivious of what awaited her. Like the other villagers, until she was chosen as tribute, she worked in the fields harvesting whatever crops we allowed her kind to grow. She is familiar with golden wheat and the dark green of corn stalks and paler green of vines. When she was toiling the ash-rich soil, did she ever wonder how many other shades of green her masters denied her through fire?

It is the promise of more, of a full verdant landscape, that gives the humans hope. It is what compels them to give us their daughters. Hope. It is almost as strong an incentive as fear. They hope that if they obey, we will give them more than protection. They hope we will burn fewer acres, will again allow trees to bloom and grass grow. And perhaps we will. But not yet. Not until our numbers are sufficiently increased.

No man or creature is immune from challenges. We need human females to propagate our own kind. The men we have conquered and left fractured and kingless do not know that we are reliant on them. We keep the mountains between us. It is only our might we allow them to see.

"Mama?"

She is murmuring in her sleep. She is dreaming. She is calling for her mother. My cock flexes and my arms ache to hold her, to comfort her.

"Oh, Mama." She says it again, her tone mournful.

"You could wake her." Zelki enters the bedchamber carrying a horn of ale leftover from the celebration that began this day in the great hall. Now he uses it to gesture towards my woman on the bed. "Unless you want me to wake her for you."

"That depends," I say, "on whether you want another scar."

My brother, young and full of hubris and humor, looks at his arm. Our kind heals quickly. The deep gash that had elicited a roar of pain has already knitted itself together. All that remains is a silver-pink line across the bulge of his upper bicep. I cannot fault him for raking his hungry gaze over the sleeping human. I cannot fault him for the cockstand that raises the front of his leather skirt. But tolerance has its limits, even for a beloved brother.

"Out Zelki!" I can hear the rumble in my voice.

In my agitated state, it would be easy to awaken the beast that lies coiled in my veins, but I must control it. The dragon inside me is eager to defend his right to the virgin on the bed. The man in me is eager to fuck her. My brother is jealous that I will be her first. He should not be. Yes, I will be the first to put my hands on her, but there is a price to pay for being first. It leaves no time for wooing, not with a kingdom waiting to celebrate. It is my job to prepare her, to rid her of her virginity. There will be time for me to woo her, later.

My brother leaves.

I walk to the bed.

Chapter Three

LYLA

I'm not dead.

I thought I was. I saw my mother's face before me, weeping. But it's faded, and I realize now that I was having a vision, a dream.

Where am I?

I'm somewhere warm. Somewhere soft. A bed, a bed larger than my bedchamber at home. The posts that support it are carved with strange, ornate symbols. I look down at my arms, my legs.

I am not dead.

But I am naked.

I reach for a blanket, and just as I pull it to my chest, he comes into view — the largest man I've ever seen. He is standing halfway across the room, watching me. His stance is purposeful, his eye intense under his dark brows. His beard, black as coal, is plaited into a point. His hair, black as his beard, hangs in a thick braid down his muscular back. His chest is broad and bare. He wears only a leather skirt. The men in my village were modest, and wore long linen shirts and pants perpetually stained by ash. I should be insulted that he has walked in, so under-clothed, to gaze upon my nakedness. But I am too grateful to be indignant.

"Are you the one who saved me?" I ask.

"Saved you?"

"From the dragon."

He smiles. His lips are full, his teeth white in his tanned face.

"Yes, the dragon. As fearsome a beast as ever lived." He walks to the bed and puts a hand on one of the posts. "Were you afraid, little one? When you first saw it, what went through your mind?"

I clutch the cover to my chest. The man is staring at me. Something about his eyes ring familiar. But that's impossible. I've never seen him before. I struggle to answer his question.

"First, that my life was over. Then..." I summon the memory of the moment the dragon's massive head rose above the lip of the ledge, the sheer size of it. "And then, I thought it was the most terrible, beautiful thing I have ever seen."

The corners of his mouth curve into a smile.

"You are a brave girl. What do they call you?"

"Lyla.

"Lyla." He repeats my name, as if tasting it.

"Did you save me?" I ask again. "What happened? It took me...in its claw..." I curl my hand, subconsciously mimicking it. I close my eyes, trying to recall more. "I do not know what happened next."

"And you do not need to." His voice is deep. It seems to rumble from within. His accent is strange to my ears. "All that matters is that you are safe. And mine."

"Yours?" I twist my hands into the sheet I clutch at my breast.

"Why, yes, little one." He moves to the side of the bed. By the gods, he is *huge*! His thighs, smooth and brown, bulge with muscles as he walks. My heart begins to flutter in my chest at his approach. "You are here, unscathed," he says. "Do you not think I deserve a boon for that?"

"A boon?" I try to swallow my nervousness. I'd planned for death, but not for this. My mind races as it sinks in what he wants. "My mother," I begin. "She will be so glad to know that I'm alive. She could give you..." My voice falters and I look around. What could my poor mother give this man whose bed is larger than a room in my house. My gaze falls on the rich tapestries on the wall, the sumptuous furs on the stone floor.

He leans over, puts a finger under my chin. His eyes lock onto mine. The irises are green, then gray, then gold. "*You* are the boon." The words are carried on hot breath scented with spiced wine. I am transfixed, unable to look away.

He wants me. I look wildly around this huge room, wondering how I went from a dragon's grip to these soft sheets, naked before a man boldly announcing his intention to deflower me. I want answers, but the eyes looking at me are stern, demanding.

"Am I to have no say?"

He cups my chin in his hand, continuing to stare me in the eye as he shakes his head. "Tell me, little one. Do you not even want to know the name of the man who will take your innocence?"

I don't immediately answer. I know that life is often unfair to women. In my village, marriages are arranged. Had I stayed, and not entered the order, I would have ended up the wife of a laborer or a farmer. I went to the Altar Rock prepared to meet my fate. I expected to die. I am alive. If it is my fate to lie beneath this stranger rather than die in the mouth of a dragon, I must accept it, for I know I can no more fight this man than fight the dragon. I will be brave. But I will know who is taking my virginity.

"Who are you?" I ask.

"I am Lord Drorgros of Fra'hir, firstborn son of Rymoth the Great, blessed be his spirit." He puts his huge hand on his chest. "You are in the Drakoryan Empire."

This means nothing to me. A lord? I thought him to be a warrior.

He climbs onto the bed. He's on his knees, and in my seated position my head barely comes above his navel. I feel like a child next to him. His hand moves to the cover I'm using to shield my body. I watch as his huge fingers curl over the top of it. I try to clutch the cover tighter, but I know I can't stop him from pulling it away. I'm right. Lord Drorgros rips it from me so roughly that I fall forward. When I start to cross my arms over my chest, he catches my wrists.

"No," he says, pulling my arms away from my body. "I will look upon my prize."

"Prize?" I'm puzzling at the word as his gaze caresses my body. He moves the back of his hand across my shoulder, pushing aside my hair. I've never been touched by a man. I freeze, feeling a shiver run through my body as he slides the hand down, watching its trajectory as it moves over the swell of my breast. The breath catches in my throat as the backs of his fingers stop just above the ruddy circle surrounding my nipple. I look up to see him studying my reaction.

"I'm going to fuck you, Lyla. Do you know what that means?"

"It means..." I start to tell him what I know of fucking, but it isn't much and I don't know how to put it into words. He reaches for his leather skirt and pulls it aside, revealing a huge, hard appendage jutting from his body.

"Do you know what this is?"

"It's a cock." I say the word quietly, the utterance sending a flush of embarrassment into my face.

I've heard the word whispered among women, often accompanied by sighs or tittering giggles. I know it goes between a woman's legs, to plant a man's seed. It's how babies are made. I've always wondered at how a baby could come out of such a small hole, but now I'm just as mystified as I watch his cock rise from a nest of dark curls, bobbing like a living thing. It seems equally impossible that such a thing could fit there, either.

"I'm afraid," I say.

He ruffles my hair as one might a child and chuckles. "Sweet little innocent. You take wonder in a dragon that could cause you hurt and fear the thing that can bring you pleasure?"

I drag my eyes away from the mighty cock jutting from his muscular loins.

"Pleasure?"

He reaches down, swooping me up in his arms. "Yes, pleasure."

Drorgros lifted me as if I were light as a feather. Now he lays me down as gently.

He reaches out with his huge hands, covering my breasts and I gasp again as I feel my nipples harden into peaks under his palms. He kneads the flesh of my left breast, softly at first, then with more pressure as his fingers find my right nipple, pinching it.

"Aaahhh!" My eyes widen in surprise. The pinch hurts, but is accompanied by what feels like a tug in that untouched place between my legs, where a soft throb, like a heartbeat, begins to pulse. I wriggle against it, squeeze my thighs together instinctively, and then gasp again when I realize my inner thighs are wet. All the while the huge man is looking down at me, a half-smile on his handsome, bearded face.

"Good," he says. "Very good."

"What?" I ask. "What is good?" My voice is high. I'm puzzled and scared. I try to rise, but his hand presses into my belly, keeping me prone as he stretches out beside me.

"I can smell your sweet pussy," he says. "Your virgin body is ready, aroused, giving up its first nectar. I would taste it..."

Taste it? What does he mean? I cry out. His large hands have wrenched my legs apart. His head is between them. He laps at the slickness coating my inner thighs and the throbbing in my core becomes nearly unbearable. I feel his beard, wiry and rough, against my tender skin. I feel his hot breath against the mound of my pussy. I bite my lip, trying to stifle a whimper.

What is happening to me? What magic is this man working that my body should act of its own accord? I try to will the throbbing to stop. It won't. I tell myself to close my legs; instead, I feel my thighs fall open, feel the air of the room caress the inner folds of my pussy, wet and exposed to his gaze and his touch.

And then his mouth finds my most secret spot and I scream as pleasure cuts through me like a knife blade. My body quakes, the unexpected sensation buffeting me in wave after delicious wave. His huge hands are under my bottom cheeks, squeezing. I grasp the cover, twisting it in my fists. What is he doing to me? I want to ask, but can only moan in a voice that doesn't sound like my own.

The man called Lord Drorgros slides his huge body up over mine, lightly pinning me to the bed. He moves his hand between us. I feel his fingers between my legs, touching, probing. There's a look of concentration on his face.

"Lyla," he says. "Sweet Lyla, who faced the dragon without fear. Will she be brave again?"

How does he know that I faced the dragon? The question is in the back of my mind, but is driven out by a surge of apprehension as he positions himself between my legs. I feel the bulb of his mighty cock pressing, replacing his fingers. He takes my face between his hands and looks me in the eye.

"Lyla," he says. "Look at me." It's not a request. It's an order. I stare into his eyes. Such unusual eyes, green and amber and then – as he shoves into me – gold with pupils deep as chasms. I scream, and he absorbs the sound with his mouth, swallowing it as he makes me his.

Chapter Four

DRORGROS

Gentleness is not a Drakoryan trait. The smell of this human, the taste of her...she will never know how hard it was to restrain myself, to keep from wrenching her thighs apart and shoving my cock into her. But I was gentle, for her sake. The first mating sets the tone. I fought for virgin rights not just because I longed to enjoy her first fruits of passion, but because the first mating should be handled carefully. Soon enough she will be in the beds of my brothers. They will not be so gentle.

She was unconscious when she arrived. She has fainted again, this time from reaching a different altitude. She peaked so quickly, and the shock of her passion was second only to the shock of the affect it had on me. I reflect on it now, marveling at the strength of her orgasm, the sweet rhythmic pressure as her pussy clenched the length of my cock.

I could have kept going. Having never been with a man of her kind, Lyla does not know that while human males need time to recover, Drakoryan males have no such limitations. Our cocks stay hard for as long as we like, and are as personal as our swords. And like our swords, we can wield them differently from human men. She will learn this, too, in time.

Her eyes begin to flutter open. They are blue, like water, and large, giving her a look of perpetual innocence. Her hair, the same gold color as summer wheat, spreads around her like a flaxen halo. My gaze moves downward, past her sweet breasts and soft belly to where my seed has mixed with her virgin blood, staining the ivory skin of her inner thighs a light pink. She stares at me, her expression unreadable.

"I'm ruined now," she says with quiet resignation. "When I go home, no man will have me."

Her words remind me of how unaware she is of her situation. She thinks I'm her savior, and now that I've extracted carnal payment, will take her back. She does not know how wrong she is. She worries that she will have no mate now. She does not know that instead, she will have *mates.*

I could explain, but decide it might be easier to simply show her. I rise and dip a cloth in the bowl by the bed. She flinches as I dab away the blood and seed from her legs, her still tender pussy.

"Are you too sore to walk?" I ask once I've cleaned her. I help her up from the bed. She reaches for the sheet, looks at me, flushes, and drops it.

"I'm sore, but not too sore to walk."

I walk to a trunk at the foot of the bed and open it. Inside is her first gown. My color is green. I take it from the chest. When she enters the hall wearing it, all will know that I have claimed her.

"Lift your arms," I say.

She complies and I position the gown over her head. The fabric, spun from the finest, shimmering thread, skims her curves as it slides over her like water. It clings to her as she moves, emphasizing a shapely thigh, a round buttock, a firm breast. Over the next few days she will earn other dresses, each marking her the property of a different son of Rymoth.

But she doesn't know this yet. She only knows she is in a strange place, and has just lost her virginity. She thinks her innocence was payment for her life. She thinks she is going home. She has much to learn. I hold out my hand.

"Come," I say, and she looks at me with skepticism before laying her hand in mine. It is so small, so slim, so delicate. I clasp it gently and lead her from the bedroom. I guide her slowly, letting her take in the first glimpse of the castle beyond the bedchamber.

I know it must be an overwhelming sight. There are a dozen castles in the Drakoryan empire, all carved into mountains. Ours, House Fra'hir, is among the oldest, existing nearly as long as the record of our kind. Its pinnacle houses a watchtower. From there, we can see across the great plains to the mountains that separate us from the humans we rule through fire and fear.

The southern plains, hemmed in by craggy mountain ranges, are peppered with villages inhabited by the first humans we conquered when we took this place. They were miners once, making their homes in the warrens and cave systems of these mighty mountains. We smoked them out, subjugated them, and pressed them into servitude. They offered little objection, and over the years have evolved from the stooped, small-eyed stock to become fairer and taller. They are loyal without question, a sturdy lot, the wenches good-natured and always up for a tumble. But they are not breeding stock; the witches have warned against mixing Drakoryan blood with those who serve us.

To the east and west are homes of other lords, all in castles overshadowing villages holding those who serve those houses. To the north is the largest castle belonging to King Vukurcis, who knighted my father. He rules us all from the tallest peak, which stands just to the left of the Mystic Mount where we go only to seek counsel from the Wyrd, a sisterhood of witches whose power is tied to our own. Here is also the forest edge. We hunt here on occasion, but for the most part concede rule of the forest realm to beings best able to navigate tangles of trees. A forest is no place for a dragon.

In the bottom of our mountain castle are dungeons, with chambers large enough to hold an enemy whose fire cannot prevail against the thickest walls. In between the pinnacle and dungeon are rooms – bedchambers and libraries, kitchens and bath houses, halls for banquets and council meetings.

I watch Lyla as we head down the carved stairs. She is observant, curious. This is a sign of a quick mind, and I am encouraged. The hardships of her village have made her resourceful. She is strong, a quality she will pass on to our sons.

When we leave the staircase we enter a long passage that is solid on one side but an open archway on the other. Stone archways overlooks a huge river that leads to the base of the mountain and under it to an inland sea. The solid side is painted with a mural. Lyla's eyes widen as she looks at the dragons depicted in the massive image, and now she stops and speaks for the first time since leaving the bedchamber.

She's staring at one dragon in particular — one with scales the same shade of green as the dress she wears. Lyla points at it with a shaking finger. "That's him," she says. "That's the dragon that took me." She turns to me. "Did you kill it? Is it gone?"

"It won't frighten you ever again," I reply, putting a hand on her shoulder. "I promise."

She glances at the mural, then up at me, worrying her plump bottom lip with her teeth. I ponder pulling her into an alcove, lifting her gown and fucking her once more before we reach the hall. She's still so innocent, still so unaware of how one small, feminine gesture can send hot blood coursing to my loins.

"Are you sure?"

"Positive, my little one."

I lead her on past the mural. The passage turns to dark again, illuminated now by huge candles that sputter and hiss. Up ahead I can hear sounds of merriment. The celebratory feast that began when Lyla arrived is in full swing. I take her hand, ready to reassure her, to help her absorb the surprise of what comes next.

And she is indeed surprised when we walk into a platform overlooking the hall. We enter to a roar of cries and thunderous applause from the revelers below who raise tankards and drinking horns. Some begin to slam their fists or cups onto the massive wood tables that run the length of the room, the steady beat rising to the ceiling above.

Lyla looks at me, puzzled.

"What do they celebrate?" she asks.

"You," I say. "They celebrate you."

"Me?"

I don't respond, instead directing her towards a flight of stairs that takes us down into the hall. It's the largest room in the castle; the fireplace along one wall holding entire burning trees. Rushes cover the flagstones under our feet. Massive hounds dart between tables, plucking dropped food from the floor. All the lords and soldiers from the empire in attendance, save the reclusive king; the banners of every house hang along the walls in their honor.

The cheers have turned into a cacophony. A new mate is always a cause for celebration, especially when a female is claimed into a family such as ours. Our friends celebrate not only our good fortune, but knowledge that the line of Rymoth the Great will continue now through his sons.

Hands clamp down on my back as we walk the gauntlet of celebrators, who rise from their benches as we pass. Lyla edges towards me, and I pull her close. I can only imagine how overwhelmed she still must be, how many questions she must have. Then the crowd parts and there they are. My brothers. Tythos, second oldest and arguably the bravest fighter among us. He's the most taciturn and if village wenches are to be believed, the most insatiable. There's Imryth, third-born, and the scholar of the group, the strategist. And then Zelki, the youngest, who often forgets his place. He's grown taller than I am, which worries me sometimes. He is a hothead, and a savage lover by reputation. In the fight for Lyla's favor, I prevailed – barely. He bested his other brothers and will be next to take her. I pray he will exercise some restraint for this small female so new to the carnal arts.

But Lyla does not know any of this. She does not know that over the coming days, each of my brothers will take her to his bed, our shared mate. If she catches the undisguised lust in the eyes of my siblings as I make introductions, she does not show it. She's shy, and keeps looking to me, no doubt still wondering why she is here.

"Sit," I say. "Sit." And she does. When Tythos tries to take a seat beside her, Zelki edges him aside and takes his place. Tension runs through me as I catch the brief flash in both their eyes.

A cheery maid walks by, bearing a tray laden with chunks of bread and meat and fruit. Zelki stands and grabs fistsful of food, placing them on a wooden slab in front of Lyla.

"You must be hungry," he says. "Or you should be, if my brother did his job." He smiles. "But, of course he did, or else you would not be here, wearing his color."

"His...color?" She looks back at me. "Please, Lord Drorgros, will someone tell me what's happening?"

"In time. But first you will eat." I issue the order sternly. The way my brother is looking at her, she will need the strength.

"Here," Zelki tears off a piece of meat and puts it to her lips. "Try this." When Lyla looks questioningly in my direction, I nod that she should obey him, even as I will myself to quash the jealousy I feel as Zelki's fingers touch her full lips.

I turn away, seeking Tythos and Imryth. Even amid the celebration, I know we must not allow ourselves to become completely distracted. The threats to our kingdom, and the empire, do not rest. We leave Zelki to his feeding of Lyla as we huddle together.

"Congratulations, brother." Tythos cuts his eyes in Lyla's direction. "Is she sweet as she looks?"

"Sweeter." I'm unable to contain my smile.

"I would have fought harder had I known she was so fair," he quips, and although his tone his light, I can sense honesty in it.

"I hope Zelki will be gentle," Imryth says.

"Since when has Zelki been gentle in anything?" I growl. "But don't fret. Now that I've had her, even if he isn't, she'll know what to expect."

I change the subject to diffuse the collective worry we all feel for Lyla, who continues to take hesitant nips of offered food from Zelki as he feeds her like a pet.

"What news from the borderlands?" I ask.

Tythos' expression turns grave. He's only just returned, a testament to his commitment to the Empire. Battles for first rights are brutal. He'd been scarred and tired when he departed, but he went on patrol anyway. I was hoping he'd return with good news. Now I brace myself for the worst.

"The village of Krenick, burned. All dead."

"All?"

"I saw none alive, but storms had moved in by then. It was hard to say for certain. Brother, if word gets out, and we are blamed..." His words fade away but he doesn't need to finish them.

We have punished by fire, but only by burning fields. Not since our subjugation of humans have we killed. As their rulers, we protect, laying down barriers of flame on winter nights to keep the Wolven away, or dropping baskets of seeds or stores from the sky. We rule the humans fairly, through reward and correction, demanding the occasional female for sacrifice. The humans believe the women we take are consumed. We let them think that; we have no desire to make an example of any male relative who would come after his daughter or sister. They do not know the real purpose of our taking the sacrifices. They do not know that to continue our kind, we need humans as mates.

"At least Krenick is isolated," I say. "That will keep word from getting out." I glance over at Lyla, who still looks uncertain as she eats from Zelki's hand. It could have been her village. "If this is the ShadowFell, it is indeed a dire sign."

"Who else would it be?" Tythos' tone edges into annoyance, and I understand why. He's right. It could be no one else.

"We must fortify," I say. "We must be vigilant."

Tythos nods. "Yes, or else we will be blamed on top of everything else. If the humans think we are randomly killing..." His voice trails off. The implications of what has happened will require a meeting of the council. But it can wait until after the storms, until after we have all taken our mate, until after the final step, the Deepening. I turn back, watching Zelki feed Lyla, envying him the treat he will soon savor.

Chapter Five

LYLA

My mind wants answers, but my body wants food. As much as I'd like to hold out for the former, the smell of savory meat and warm bread makes me realize how ravenous I am. I'm no stranger to hunger, but the people of my village have learned to be satisfied with little.

The man feeding me is beautiful, and while I see a resemblance to Lord Drorgros, there are differences. Even though he's bigger, the man who identifies himself as Lord Zelki is obviously younger. Where Drorgros' beard is longer and braided, Lord Zelki's is cropped short. Where Drorgros' hair is fashioned into one long plait, Zelki's raven tresses hang to his shoulders. His nose is sharper, his cheekbones higher. But the eyes – those unusual eyes – are just the same save for the expression. Zelki's eyes are bolder. His gaze makes me feel naked.

"Do you like the meat?" Zelki's mouth curls into a smile as I swallow.

"It's good," I reply, flushing under his scrutiny. "Thank you.

"Try this." Another maid walks past and he plucks what looks like a red rock from the tray. "Have you ever seen one of these?" He hands it to me. "It's delicious."

"You're teasing me," I say. "This is a stone."

He plucks it from me. "To your kind, it might as well be." He grips it between his hands and pulls. The hard skin breaks with an audible crack, revealing snow white fruit that smells of honey.

"My kind?" I ask, but he doesn't answer. Instead, he dips two fingers into the fruit and puts it in my mouth.

"Open," he commands, and I obey. He feeds me the fruit. It's so sweet, so good, that I'm speechless. "This fruit is called Bride's Melon."

"Bride's Melon?" I ask once I've swallowed. "Why?"

"I'll show you," he says with a wink. "Once we are alone."

"Alone?" I wipe away the juice from my mouth. It's left a pleasant tingle on my lips.

"Let me guess. My brother didn't tell you."

"Tell me what? If you refer to why I'm here, he hasn't."

He turns. "Drorgros!" The man whose bed I awoke in looks over. Zelki commands me to stay put and leaves me on the bench as he begins conferring with this brother. I see them glance back at me, and am piqued. I know nothing beyond the fact that I am not dead, have paid for my safety with my virginity, and was cheered when I walked in. Much is being hidden from me, and after what I have faced, I am no longer afraid. Despite being told to stay seated, I rise and walk over to the men.

"Lord Drorgros," I say. "You told me if I ate, you would give me answers." He looks at me, obviously surprised at the forcefulness of my tone. "I want them." Beside him, his brothers look from him to me, their expressions clearly bemused. I can tell by Drorgros' expression that he is not used to being challenged, and now he stands, looming over me.

"So I did," he says. "But not here. Come. We have someone who is eager to see you."

Someone who wants to see me? It seems that every time Drorgros opens his mouth, I only end up more confused. He leads me back out of the room, only this time I am flanked by his three brothers. The room is cheering again; all around us men raise tankards and beat their muscular chests or raise their fists in encouragement. But of what?

There's a door to the side and we walk through it. When it shuts, the cacophony from the hall is silenced. It's a little darker in here. As my eyes adjust to the darkness, I hear a female voice call my name.

"Lyla?"

I freeze. I know this voice. I turn and for a moment cannot breathe.

"Enid?" I sway as I speak her name, and Drorgros must have been expecting my reaction, for he moves to steady me as I stare in disbelief at the woman who moves from the shadows to walk towards me.

"You're dead," I say, my voice quavering. "I saw ..."

She takes my hands in hers. Her hands warm and very much alive. "You saw what everyone sees, Lyla. You saw what the villagers, and your mother, and the priestesses saw after *you* went to the rock. You saw a sacrificed being claimed by the dragon." She smiles. "But you did not see me die, did you?"

I turn slowly to face Drorgros. "Tell me. Tell me what this means."

"On a designated day on the Drakoryan calendar, your village sacrifices their most beautiful daughters to us..."

I shake my head. "No. We're sacrificed to the dragons."

He stares down at me. The other men are staring at me, too.

"The dragons claim you. In fact, they fight for that right, my dear. The one who proves strongest brings you here, to your new life, your new home..."

I step back. "You didn't save me?" I shake my head in disbelief, tears springing to my eyes. "*You* had me taken?" I look wildly from one brother to the other. "*You* control the beasts that burn our crops, that terrorize my people, that rip beloved daughters from weeping families...?"

Drorgros' tone is stern. "Those beasts also protect you, and gift your people with..."

But I'm not listening. I whirl on Enid. My voice is shaking as I interrupt his explanation to confront her. "How can you accept this? Do you not remember the fear? The pain? Do you not remember the sound of your mother's weeping as you were taken to the rock?"

"Yes," Enid says. Her serenity infuriates me, but she ignores the anger in my expression as she continues. "And when I first came and saw women from our village and others, I felt just as betrayed, just as angry. There is so much you are yet to understand, but all will be revealed to you by your mates." She nods her head in the direction of Drorgros and his brothers.

I look at them and back at her. "Mates?" I whisper.

"Mates," she repeats, and smiles. "The way of the Drakoryans is not our way. The men here jointly claim one woman. I belong to three brothers, and had I known how happy all of this would make me, I would have leapt into the dragon's clasp. In the village, we get one man who may be cruel or weak or impotent. But here? We get several men sworn to your care and safety. You'll never lack for attention, Lyla. You'll never be without protection. They will supply all that you need. They are fierce, but fiercely loyal. But if you are brave, my friend, that bravery will be rewarded. The bonds you form..."

Her words die away and she drops her eyes and steps back, as if fearing to reveal too much. How can she be so accepting? All this time she's been here, alive, letting us think she was dead. At home, her mother still weeps, will always weep. So will mine. I am not assuaged.

"No!" I say, shaking my head. "This can't be happening." I face Drorgros. "Why didn't you tell me?"

"We do things in our own time, our own way," comes his maddening answer. He puts a hand to my face and looks into my eyes. "You are strong, and curious. But you are, little one, also outnumbered. My brothers and I fought for you, and we will claim you in order of our victories. You must face this, just as you faced the dragon. Surely a woman who stared the beast in the eye can face men."

"How do you know I looked it in the eye?" I ask, whirling back to Drorgros. "You said that to me, in the bedchamber. You asked me how it felt. Do they talk to you, your ... *dragons*?" I spit the word, like bitter venom, from my mouth.

A shadow of a smile crosses his face. "Always."

"Show me." It's insane, I know. But I want to see. "Show me the dragon."

He ruffles my hair as if I am a child. "Soon enough, my little spitfire." Around us, the others laugh. Even Enid is suppressing a smile at my demand. "For now, Zelki has another beast he'd like you to meet."

I feel a large hand on my arm as Zelki leans down and puts his mouth to my ear. Like his brother, his breath is unnaturally warm, and despite myself I feel a shudder run down my body that is not unpleasant as he speaks. "He teases you, Lyla. I'm convinced the beast in you will be more than a match for the beast in me."

I could fight. I could run. But I am pragmatic enough to know that I have no choice. These men are using my curiosity as leverage, promising me glimpses of knowledge in exchange for my compliance. The only way to find out what I need to know is to comply, to use the only capital I have – my body.

I turn to Zelki, look right into his eyes.

"Are you taking me to your bedchamber, then?"

He grins. "Yes. But first, let me show you one of the hidden wonders of this castle."

Chapter Six

ZELKI

Just because I am the youngest does not mean I defer to my brothers as they expect. We are all lords, and while I respect my elder siblings, I believe myself to be the strongest, as father often observed I was. I should be leader. One day, I think, I will be.

I have burned inwardly for a mate for several moon cycles. Tythos said I should be thinking of other things, but with each claiming celebration, I felt jealousy. As I watched other females arrive in the great hall clad in the color of their conqueror, their eyes confused and skin flushed with sex glow, I dreamt of the day my brothers and I would claim our female, too.

I'd fully intended to win the battle for Lyla's rights. I wanted to be first. I should have been first. I'd defeated both Tythos and Imryth, and was confident I would beat Drorgros, too. But I was overly confident. I depended too heavily on my strength and speed. My eldest brother used skill, allowing me to exhaust myself in combat. I did land a few mighty blows, one of which sent him reeling. But in the end, it was I who came crashing to the ground. It was I who crawled off into a cave, and curled up to heal.

Now, my time has come, and I will not spend it ruminating over a loss. I can still be the victor in all of this. I will prevail in this female's mind as the most masterful lover. I will ruin her for the others. After tonight, she will think of me, even when she is with them.

But first, a surprise. I can tell she's apprehensive as I lead her down a dark stairwell. We are heading deep into the castle, deeper into the mountain. The walls are damp; the candles lighting the way sputtering in the moist air. If we kept going, we would eventually reach the dungeons. I will not take her there. It is a dark place, the bone-littered floor reserved for enemies.

Instead, we turn left into a narrow passage. I take Lyla's hand, feeling the reluctance in her gait. I do not allow her to stop. I move steadily, eager to introduce her to the hidden pleasures of the realm.

There are many pools under these mountains, but none as fine as the Pools of Fra'hir. When we enter the cavern, she stops in her tracks, her sweet little mouth a moue of surprise. I say nothing, stepping back as she takes in the towering, iridescent stalagmites that rise to border multiple pools over varying depths. Stalactites hang from the ceiling. She looks back at me.

"They remind me of teeth," she says. "Teeth of the dragon."

"But not as lethal." I point to the hanging and rising points made of sediment laid down over millennia.

"They shimmer, like the dragon's scales."

"That dragon must have made quite an impression on you," I say, feeling a bit jealous that she would mention him, when here with me. But she doesn't yet understand.

"Come." I take her hand and lead her to the pool. I kneel, touching the water. As my hand ripples the surface, tendrils of steam rise to curl above our heads.

"You're tired?" I ask. "Still sore?" When she drops her eyes, I smile at her shyness. "There is no need to be bashful. Your sweet little sex is freshly opened. Of course you are still tender. Come. Take your gown off."

"Why?" Bashfulness turns to trepidation.

"Because I am your mate, and I command you to obey me."

I can see the pulse dancing in her throat. I can sense she is considering the consequences of defying my direct order. I take a step towards her. She takes a step back.

"I could rip it from you," I say. "But it would offend my brother. A female gets a gown representing the color of each of her mates. Should I have to tear Drorgros' gift, he will be angered."

She glares at me, and after a moment reaches for her shoulder, pushing the fabric from first the left and then the right. I watch as the gown slides off, leaving her naked. Her eyes are on the floor, her body flushed from her modesty. I look forward to helping her shed that modesty just as she shed the dress. But first, the pool. She needs stamina for what I have in store.

I strip now. She averts her gaze. It's charming, and makes me want her more. I wade into the pool. "Come," I say. "Swim with me."

"I don't know how to swim."

I crook two fingers, beckoning her towards me. "I won't let you drown. Come."

She walks to the rim and stands there.

"It looks hotter than it is. Step in."

Lyla glances at me skeptically and then dips her toe in. Gasping, she pulls it back, then dips it in again, sinking this time up to her foot. Her eyes meet mine and I can see the wonder in them. She has both feet in now, taking small steps.

"This is unbelievable," she says, and smiles, forgetting her fear.

"They're called the Revival Baths. Not every castle has them, and of the ones that do, ours are the finest. Warriors come here to heal. How do you feel?"

"I feel...awake," Lyla says. "And the soreness..." She's up to the tops of her thighs now and puts a hand to her lower belly as she blushes.

"Gone?" I ask. "Good. You'll need these springs again tomorrow. They are popular with newly claimed females."

I push myself backward, stroking through the healing waters, watching as she wades deeper. Ours healing pools are the strongest in the land, save for the one in the Mystic Mount. That one is rumored to be powerful enough to raise the dead, and is jealously guarded by its keepers.

Lyla sinks in up to her waist, then lower. She closes her eyes as she lifts her blonde hair. She is a vision of beauty, luxuriating in the pool, her breasts bobbing on the surface of the water, their nipples beckoning me. My cock stiffens and lifts, straining towards her, acting now like a living thing that would pull me forward if it could.

"Are all the pools like this?" she asks, glancing across the massive cavern.

I tell her no, that there are different ones, although I do not elaborate. Eventually she will learn the different pools, and their purposes. There are ones for bathing; the minerals in the waters replenishing human skin and leaving it silky soft. There are the birthing springs, where – once a year – some human females choose to deliver our young. Then there are the dream springs with heady steams that, when inhaled, induce visions. Those are reserved for the rare girl child born to our kind, whose power is tested in those waters before they are sent to join the witches.

"Come," I say. "You're still new to the pools. They do more than reinvigorate; they also heighten the senses. If you stay any longer, every little noise and smell will be a distraction. You may not be able to sleep for days."

I can tell she doesn't want to leave. We must supervise the humans – both mates and servants – lest some become addicted to the waters. Years ago, my father was forced to station a guard at the door when a servant insisted on sneaking in. So energized did the servant become that he refused all food and sleep. He eventually died, consumed from the inside by boundless energy as his body starved. I tell Lyla this as she steps from the water, and she nods.

She's a vision on the edge of the pool, but when she leans down to pick up her discarded gown, I stop her.

"No," I say, climbing from the water. I snatch up her dress and toss it on a nearby rock before clothing myself. "It's time to leave."

"You'd have me walk unclothed?" She is indignant.

"It pleases me," I say. "But do not worry. In my company, no other will dare lay his eyes upon you." And it is true. As we head back through the castle halls, everyone we pass instantly turns their backs to us in deference to my position and my mate's privacy. Only Lyla's mates can look upon her nakedness, and we are a possessive lot. My making her walk naked is by design. I want her to understand how safe she is in our presence now, want her to know that she could walk anywhere — even naked — and be protected because she is ours, because all within the walls of this castle, nay, this kingdom, know better than to touch the mate of a Drakoryan.

Still, I can tell it is hard for her, and I share her relief when we finally arrive at my bedchamber. Here, I will put my stamp on her.

The servants have left food and wine on the table. I pour a glass, and take it to her.

"Drink," I say. "It's the finest in the empire. Volcanic soil makes for the best grapes. The ones we grow are as big as your little hand." I lift her hand and mold her fingers around the stem of the glass. "Bigger, I think."

She regards me for a moment before taking a sip. "It's delicious."

"Another." I'm watching her mouth, her lips where the wine tinges them. I imagine those lips open in a moan, or wrapped around my cock. I must have her. This is enough courting for me. I take the glass away.

"Are your lips as sweet as the wine? Let me taste." I lean down and put my finger under her chin, tilting her head back. My lips meet hers, parting them. I sweep the honeyed cavern of her mouth with my tongue, tasting her sweetness mingled with the wine.

As my tongue tangles with her, I undo the clasp of my belt, sending my leather garment falling to the floor. I take her hand, guiding it to my cock. I mold her fingers around it, just as I molded them around the wine glass, and she cries out, pulling her head away.

"It moves!" she cries, pulling her hand away as well, and I laugh.

"Of course it does. See how it stiffens for you, little Lyla?"

She retreats a few steps, pointing at me. "No. Not like that. Not like your..." She flushes. "Not like your brother's. I felt something different with yours, something under the skin."

"Did you now? You are a very observant female to notice so quickly. Come. Let me show you how different one brother is from another."

But she shakes her head, staring at my cock, for now it's clear she sees the difference she felt. "No." Her voice is quavering. "I'm not ready."

"Worry not," I reply. "I will ready you. And then, I will drive you mad."

Chapter Seven

LYLA

I'd thought it was my imagination. When Lord Zelki wrapped my hand around his cock, at first it had felt like his brother's. It was warm and hard and firm, evoking a flashback to the rushes of ecstasy that has coursed through my body when he'd impaled me.

And then I felt it — the surface, bulging, undulating, as if something was moving beneath the skin. I am not an experienced woman, not yet. But instinctively I knew this was not normal, that if it were, I'd have caught some whispers of it from the wives of my village. Then, as I backed away, I'd seen it. His huge cock, pointing straight at me, had bulged and flexed before my eyes.

I am still objecting when Zelki lays his hands on me again. He closes his mouth over mine, swallowing my half-hearted protestations, for the insistence of his kiss sends heat coursing through me; despite my fear, my body is already betraying me — my nerves set alight by the nearness of this powerful man, so beautiful, so virile, so ... demanding.

I try to tamp down the excitement, but his hand moves between my legs now, his palm closing over the mound of my outer labia before he drags a finger up through my dewy slit. I jolt at the sensation; his touch is insistent, but so light as to send a shiver through my body.

"You are a passionate little thing," he murmurs into my hair, and when my knees grow weak from his touch, he lifts me from the floor and carries me to his bed.

His bedchamber is as large as Drorgros', but nearly every inch of the stone floor is covered with some kind of fur. I recognize the pelts of a giant Wolven, and a Night Bear - beasts that can kill with one bite or swipe of their mighty paws. There are other furs, too — unrecognizable pelts of animals from a world that is bigger than I ever realized.

Zelki lays me on the bed and stands over me. His huge hands roam my body, his touch possessive. He clasps my breasts, squeezing them, and leans down, the hot suction of his mouth on my nipple causing me to cry out and arch upward from the bed. I am forced to wrap my arms around his neck, and hang there, crying out at the rhythmic pull of his mouth, so hot, so demanding. He thrusts two fingers into my pussy, meeting a flow of arousal that eases their entry into my welcoming body.

"I don't want this!" I say through gritted teeth, but I'm speaking to myself, not him, in a bid to win back control of my traitorous body. What have these men done to me that I should so easily play the whore? My legs are spread, my hips rising to meet Zelki's fingers. There's no pain now, thanks to the healing waters. There is only excitement, and a burning want to be filled.

When he releases my nipple, I sink back down onto the bed, gasping. Zelki smiles, and reaches for the bedside table. "Remember this?" He holds up the fruit he fed me in the hall, the one with the skin like a red rock, the one called Bride's Melon. Just as he did in the hall, he cracks it open with his bare hands. But this time he drizzles the juice over my breasts, then between them, down to the top of my cleft. He lowers his head, his mouth follows the line of juice. My skin tingles where the juice fell. I begin to squirm. The tingle seems to sink below my skin, making my body thrum. Zelki dips is finger into the fruit, and when I realize what he intends, I try to pull away. But he's too fast. I cannot take this. I will not be able to stand it. I cry out as he slides the fruit into my body. It dissolves inside of pussy just as it did in my mouth. The juice mingles with my own arousal, sliding from my pussy down to the crinkle of my bottom hole. I am alight, tingly and suddenly all I can think of his being filled, of having my tingling passage touched, stroked, *fucked*. I am writhing on the bed, desperate for relief. I slide my hands between my legs, but Zelki catches them, clasping them at my side.

"No," he says. "No."

He flips me over, shoving my head down onto the bedcovers as he pulls my hips roughly back and up. My ass is in the air. I feel his mouth on my labia. I scream. His tongue feels large, magnified. I push back as he laps at my pussy, licking away the mingling juices. His finger has moved to my bottom hole. I want to move away, but instead, I push back as he moves over top of me. I *want* this. I want it more than I can say.

"Let go," he growls in my ear. "Let me see you fly."

He shoves his cock into me. I look back, passion-drunk, my vision hazy. His cock seems thinner as it enters, but once inside me, I remember how it had felt to touch him, what I'd seen. When he begins to move, I remember his words. He promised me pleasure, but this is beyond pleasure. He moves inside me, seeking. Then he stops moving, or at least his hips do. His cock continues to move inside me, pulsing in one spot to caress a secret, internal source of pleasure that seems a hundred times more sensitive than the external bud he so masterfully stroked with his tongue.

I scream into the covers as he holds my hips and begins to move his hips again, the bulge on his cock caressing that single spot with each thrust. Rushes of pleasure ripple through me. He is fucking he hard, one hand fisted into my hair, one hand on my hip. I can't move. I can only absorb the impact of his feral barrage of savage strokes as I scream my pleasure.

Zelki is using me, dominating me completely. I am helpless, subjugated, but I love it. He's forced me to submit, and that submission has awakened something feral inside me.

I scrabble to all fours, reach back, raking his side with my nails. He laughs, pulls out, throws me on my back and shoves into me from above. I wrap my arms around his neck. This time it is my hands in his hair. I tangle my fingers in the raven strands as I move with him, meeting his thrusts. I feel detached from my body, which I realize has its own innate knowledge of this primal dance, is communicating with Zelki's in a language older than the mountain. I hear a scream and realize it is mine as I come, my pussy pulsing and drawing hard on Zelki's cock, demanding the release of seed that floods into me. I arch against him. His body is hot; I imagine myself seared to him, being absorbed, consumed. I have not felt this kind of power since the dragon took me off the mountain. I have never felt anything like this.

When Zelki stops moving, his cock stays lodged in my pussy, the length of it engorged.

"I don't want to let you go," he says, and now his voice and mannerisms are surprisingly tender, a sea change from the ravishing lord. I can feel my body start to settle, to return to normal. The fiery nerve endings are cooling. I relax, sinking into the bed under his warm, muscular form. His eyes, so like his brother's, study me. I stare into them. Although Zelki is young, his eyes are not. They have seen things. Know things. I am certain of this.

He lifts himself up on his elbows, staring down at me.

"Did you see the furs on the floor?" he asks.

I nod.

"Wolven. Night Bears. Cave Tigers that could swallow a little thing like you whole. I slew them all with only a knife. I have fought my brothers and defeated all save one. Outside my family, I have never been defeated." He pauses. "Until today. I came into this bedchamber to master you, Lyla. When I said the beast in me would meet my match in you? That was to play to your vanity. But you, my wild little lover, have put me in my place. You, Lyla, Drakoryan Mate, Bride of the Lords of Fra'hir, are unlike any other female."

"Have you had many other females?" I ask, studying his face in the firelight.

He grins. "Hundreds. We all have, save for Tythos. He's had thousands." Zelki winks at me. "But no more. We are yours now. No other female will do for us, and we would all die to keep you happy and safe and cared for."

"How can you know that?" I ask.

He lays on his back, pulling me up on top of him. I'm straddling him now, looking down on him. Zelki stares up at my breasts and puts an arm behind his head.

"Because I am the strongest, the bravest, and the best among my brothers, and yet I lay here, your willing slave."

I flush at his words. Is he teasing me, or have I conquered this man merely by submitting to him?

"My slave?" I say. "So, you would do anything?"

"Name it."

I lean over and place my palms on the huge mounds of his pectorals. "Very well. I want to see the dragon."

Chapter Eight

ZELKI

My brothers would not approve of this. There is a protocol we are deemed to follow. Knowledge is revealed piecemeal, in digestible bites so as not to overwhelm a freshly taken mate. It starts with the initial claiming by the victor. Slowly, she's given more insight. Glimpses of the castle, the hall, the others who will claim her, then the revelation that she is not alone. Enid was one of those revelations. The dragons? They are the last, after the consummations, after the Deepening which brings full understanding.

But she wants to see one now, and I have decided to share this with her, secretly. I can do this without revealing the whole of the truth.

I find a shift for her to wear. It is thin and gauzy, and through it I can see the shape of her breasts, her narrow waist, the belly that will one day swell with a Drakoryan son. But I get ahead of myself. There are two brothers yet to claim her before the Deepening.

I was afraid Enid would speak of it, that she would tell Lyla too much. Fortunately, she did not. Perhaps Drorgros raised a brow, warning her to be quiet. Perhaps one of Enid's mates, sensing the conversation, whispered to her mind that she'd said enough. It is not for a Sister to reveal the mysteries to a newcomer. That is the right of her mates alone.

I know I am out of order, with what I am about to show her. We climb staircase after staircase, walking upwards through spiral hallways. We pass a storeroom. Lyla is looking ahead to the next bend, and away from the doors with their small grated window. Had she stopped to glance in one, she'd have seen treasure piled to the ceiling. The upper reaches of the castle are full of such rooms. Other rooms, deeper below the mountain, hold even more treasure — spoils of conquered kingdoms. Our kind has little need of the glittering rubies, the cold coins and goblets and ornate shields. We hoard them only because we realize their value to the fully human. Man's reliance on such trinkets is yet another of their weaknesses. One day, should we relax our grip and restore some of their power, we can reward the humans with what they prize.

"How much longer?"

We've been climbing for a very long time, and Lyla has started to tire. Had she not been to the pool, she might have collapsed already.

"A way, yet," I say. "I'll carry you." I lift her over her objections, cradling her in one of the furs I picked up before we left my room. She's light and warm in my arms. "Put your arms around my neck, Lyla."

She complies, and the feel of her clinging to me rouses a protectiveness nearly as strong as my sexual urge for her. I could easily see myself killing to protect her, keep her. And suddenly, I hate my brothers. I hate Drorgros for having had her. I hate Tythos and Imryth, who now await their turn.

I was warned of this. Once a year, the Oracle journeys to the Mystic Mountains, where the witches divine which houses will be allowed to select a mate. He returns with advice for the Drakoryan males who are given permission to mate. We are told which strengths we will bring to the relationship, and which weakness. Mine is jealousy, and anger. I am feeling my weakness. I must master it, before it masters me. She is not mine. She is *ours*. I must remember that.

I can feel the wind. I can hear it. It whistles from the top, from the uppermost watchtower above the Oracle's room. Lyla grips me tighter as the wind gets stronger. When we emerge onto a narrow, spiral stone staircase outside the walls, she gasps in fear. The steps are slick with ice and snow this high up, and the gusts so strong they would easily knock down an average human male.

I must keep her warm. I close my eyes, uncoiling the beast inside me just enough to raise my body temperature, warming her as I climb. Finally, at the top we emerge onto a platform with a peaked stone roof. From here, we see nothing but mountains. From here, we see to the ends of the world. I set her down, draping the fur over her shoulders. I point to the north.

"Wait," I say.

We wait. It is late in the Long Day. The sun is sinking ever so slowly in the sky, a giant blazing ball of orange. In her village, she'd already be in bed. But magic is employed here to shift time. Nights are brief in the wake of a claiming, the days longer.

A gust of wind blows so hard that Lyla closes her eyes against it. When she turns back to face the north, she tenses and gasps. I know she has seen the silhouette before, that even from this distance the small speck over the mountain could trigger the most traumatic memory of her life.

I ready my arms to open, to hold her should she turn away in fear. Instead, she steps away from me and rushes to the railing before I can stop her. The dragon, which had folded its wings to ride an air channel down to the opening in the mountain, now spreads them to brake, blotting out the sun. I jerk her back.

"No!" she cries, fighting me. "I want to see!"

It is not her bravery that concerns me. My worry comes from realizing the dragon, red as the sunset behind it, has seen us. Nostrils that extruded smoke now inhale, pulling in surrounding smells — her smell. And the eye, having gone gray to yellow, is fixed on me, and narrowing as, behind him, more dragons appear on the horizon.

"Come, Lyla," I say, and am grateful when the dragon loops and dives out of sight. "We must go."

"Why?"

"Because I am wanted in the council room."

"How do you know?"

I turn her to me, grasping her shoulders. I'm angry, not at her, but at myself. Weakness. My desire to cleave her to me, to reveal something special and secret out of natural order, has now angered my brothers. In my mind, I can hear them, already summoning me.

"You ask too many questions," I snap. "You wanted to see a dragon. I showed you a dragon."

I scoop her up. I can feel her fuming. The sighting has left her even more frustrated. And although we've not achieved the Deepening, I already know what she's thinking. She wants to know why they are here, how we control them, why we sent them. She wants to know so many things.

I head towards the chamber we've set aside just for her, knowing she must rest before going back to the hall. I will use the time to talk to my brothers, to sort this out. Beti, a trusted nurse, is waiting by the chamber door.

"I've been told to take her in," she says.

"Thank you," I reply, and set Lyla back on her feet. She looks up at me, glaring.

"So, I'm to be locked away, am I?"

"Yes." I'm firm. "For now. But I will be back. Go on now."

She looks towards the open door, as if considering once again whether to defy me. I feel my cock stiffen at the thought of taking her into the chamber, of pushing her onto the bed, of reminding her once more of my ability to conquer her. Then I remember her power, her intoxicating sweetness, how she turned the tables without even trying, leading to a rash decision that has put me on the outs with my brethren.

"Go," I say one more time, allowing my heat to rise. My voice changes as my inner beast uncoils. It is deep, and she is unnerved. She goes inside. Her nurse follows, and shuts the door.

Chapter Nine

TYTHOS

Foolish, foolish, pup!

I am slow to anger, but as I pace the hall waiting for Zelki to show himself, I find it hard to control my growing rage. Imryth rises and walks with me. I know he seeks to calm me with his presence. He has always been the peacemaker. When the ship of our family begins to drift, his calm is the ballast.

"He knows better," I boom, my voice ricocheting around the round room. Drorgros is sitting at the table, slumped slightly, with his head resting in his hand.

"Zelki has always been impetuous," Imryth says. "He likely just wanted to impress her."

"No. It's more than that." I'm seething. "He seeks advantage, favor. If that is not the case, let him deny it to our faces."

"And what if I did?"

Our youngest brother storms in, and what did I expect? Contrition? Humility? If he felt any shame for what he's done, he's hiding it now beneath his ever-present layer of hubris.

He walks over to me. He's as tall as Drorgros now, and stands face to face with me, knowing I must cast my eyes slightly upwards now to meet his. "If you are the kind of lover you are famed to be, Tythos, surely the workings of your mighty cock will eclipse the small favor I did for Lyla."

His words drip with mockery, but I sense something deeper.

"Is that why you did it, then, Zelki? For fear that I'd drive you from her mind? You try so hard to hide the truth from us, but I don't need to search the channels of your mind to know that you seek to prove yourself superior in everything, even in the taking of our mate."

"And why shouldn't I?" Zelki throws his hands up and walks to a table along the wall, pouring himself a horn of wine. "I am the strongest. Even father acknowledged it…"

"Father is dead." Drorgros' deep voice booms through the hall. "And he praised all our strengths at one time or another, Zelki. My leadership, Tythos' bravery in war, Imryth's knack for strategy. You were the only one to take father's praise as some kind of call to arms against your brothers." He rises, shoving his chair away. "I grow weary of this, little brother. We are *not* your enemies. Our enemies our out there." He points to the window. "You'd be wise to remember that."

"Especially now." Olin the Wise has a voice soft and thin as mist, but just his whisper demands attention. He's been standing in the corner of the room, where he often hovers, undetected, during any gathering. Most of the time he listens, taking the information back to the crooked, book-laden room at the top of the castle, where he divines with runes and pyromancy, and inhales smoke from burning herbs as he trance-talks with the witches.

Now he points a bony finger at my younger brother. "Have a care, young Zelki. This woman who has been chosen to mate with the sons of Rymoth of Fra'hir could easily end your house should you forget your place."

Our youngest brother, so swelled with bravado only a moment ago, deflates under the oracle's withering stare.

"You've seen something?" Imryth asks, and Olin tilts his head.

"Yes, and Zelki should take heed. You all should. Your new mate is a female of powerful appetites that extend far beyond physical passion. She is a seeker, your Lyla, and this will serve you after the Deepening. But her will to know will challenge you, too. She is no amenable mate, this one. She will not be content with the mere pleasures of the bedchamber, not impressed with your strengths, your protection, mighty though may be. Take care, all of you, not to underestimate this human woman. I have seen only one such mate before. Ages ago — before you were even a thought — there was Arvika, a fierce human whose blood runs through the veins of kings now."

"Arvika?" Drorgros furrows his brow. "My father spoke of her as legend. She was the only human to transcend her station as Drakoryan mate. Surely you don't mean..."

"Yes," Olin says. "The Queen of the Witches."

Drorgros chuckles. "You compare our little human to Arvika?"

"You dare doubt me?" There is a thread of steel in Olin's misty voice. And if my eldest brother doubts him, the quickest mind among us does not. Imryth turns to Drorgros.

"If we doubt Olin's counsel, can we really scold Zelki? We are being urged to caution here. Olin the Wise has never been wrong, not with us, not with father. We should take heed." Imryth turns his attention to the Oracle. "What would you have us do?"

"Take her," Olin replies. " And quickly. There are two of you left. Acknowledge her curiosity, but not in a way that would hint at empty flattery. She will not forgive you for that. The sooner you all consummate your union, the sooner the Deepening will take place. She already seeks the truth. But only then will she be ready for it, and for her connection to it." He looks at Zelki. "Do not allow her to divide you. She may do so, not for spite, perhaps not even on purpose, but this is a strong-willed female. She may use your arrogance against you without even trying."

He pulls aside his hood then and we glimpse his face, the skin parchment-thin and creased with lines, the nose hooked like an eagle's beak, the eyes pale blue. He is having a vision, and the shock of it casts us into stunned silence. We rarely see Olin's face; rarer still do we get a message through him. When he opens his mouth, another voice comes out, a female voice, that is not his own.

"Dark times are head, sons of Rymoth of House Fra'hir. The ShadowFell have awakened, and they are coming. Their motivations this time are worse and more powerful than anything you can imagine.

"Heed the words of our vessel, Olin the Wise. Trifle not with your mate; she will be your powerful ally. Fight not for her favor; it will divide your energies. Trust that she can supply each of you with the full of what you need. Trust her instincts, for they come from a place of hidden power. Doubt not her capacity for love, for loyalty, for passion. Guard her. Keep her. Protect her. For one day, you will follow her as she will follow you."

The room falls silent. The blue haze that had clouded Olin's eyes disappears. He blinks, as if confused, and sways. I rush forward and take him by the elbow, steadying him.

"Easy, old fellow," I say.

He looks around, disoriented, and then glances at me, bashful. "Bah." He waves a dismissive hand. "I am fine."

Still, he lets me lead him to a chair and help him to sitting as Zelki puts the horn of wine to the thin old lips. Olin sips, swallows, and leans back with a sigh.

"What did she say?" he asks. "I felt her come into me. It must be urgent, if she spoke here, now..."

Our eyes meet over the Oracle's head.

"She confirmed our worst fear," I reply. "The ShadowFell have awoken. She said they plan something dire."

"Did she say what?"

"No," Drorgros says. "But there was something of a prophecy, about Lyla."

"Yes," the Oracle says. "They have been sending me small messages, through the runes and in the Telling Flames. She is to be more than a mother of sons, they say."

"So, she is to rule over us, then?" Zelki's tone is curt and clipped.

Drorgros smirks. "It seems to me she is already leading at least one of us without even trying."

"You arrogant..."

"Enough!" Imryth is scowling. "Is this what we're doing now? Bickering like old housemaids on the heels of advice to pull together? Or do you think the witches were using Olin as a vessel for their amusement?"

"He's right." Zelki speaks, and I'm surprised at how humbled he is. "I should not be so prideful." He glances at our eldest brother. "Or so reckless." He turns to me. "You are next. I am sorry that I have caused strife ahead of your time with Lyla. I admit it. I was jealous. Jealous and...perhaps afraid. I thought if I let her see a dragon..." He looks suddenly bashful, chastened, like the younger brother who tagged after us as a child. "I wanted to give her something special. I know it was wrong. There's always been plenty for all of us, of everything.

And yet here we are, having to share the one thing that we're naturally inclined to want for ourselves."

I nod along with my brothers. I do understand. I have been with more females than my brothers combined. I have fucked my way through the empire, tumbling housemaids in my castle and the castles of others. They have all spread their legs willingly, all eager to brag of being taken by the randiest of Rymoth's sons. I've taken them three, four, five at a time, leaving them so spent they could barely crawl from the bed. Today, that all ends. When a Drakoryan takes a mate, he is cleaved to her and no other. The idea of ending the wondrous variety of females at my disposal has made me resentful. Olin says Lyla will be enough. I have seen her; she is indeed fair. But I have a difficult time believing one woman can satisfy me, not even if I heard it in a hundred prophecies.

"Once Zelki celebrates his mating in the Hall, you will go to her," Drorgros says.

I nod. "And how will you three pass the time while I bed this little wench?"

"I could scout," Imryth says. "See if I can detect any border breaches."

"No," Drorgros says firmly. "It may not be safe."

"I'll be careful." Imryth, who has the leaner build and light eyes of our mother, scowls. "I could take Bartax."

"No." Drorgros shakes his head. "We will not risk either of you. Until the weather breaks, it is useless. Besides, Enid will not thank you if you go off with one of her mates and get him killed."

"I would get no one killed," Imryth says. "You heard Olin. We have to act."

"Yes." Olin speaks again. "But thoughtfully. We have a prophecy to consider. Although we do not know what role Lyla will play, she is at the core, but only as a consummated partner. If you were to be injured before the Deepening, it could ruin everything. Once a prophecy has been revealed we must bring our will in line with its path."

I can tell that Imryth is not pleased. As second to the youngest, he is the intellectual in our family, the strategist with as much faith in his mind as Zelki has in his muscle. If he sees a problem, he is impatient to work on it. If there is intelligence to be gathered, he wants to be the one gathering it.

But he's sensible, and more inclined to obey Drorgros, who — for all practical purpose — has assumed the role that our father vacated in death. We look to him, even if it is begrudgingly.

"We will abide here until all have taken Lyla. We will abide here until the Deepening. The ShadowFell will be there, waiting, when we are done."

Chapter Ten

LYLA

How long have I slept? I do not know.

I was more angry than tired when Beti led me into a different chamber, presumably one set aside just for me, with walls of pinkish stone. The bed here is beautiful, albeit smaller, the four posts carved to twist up and over like heavy wooden vines. There's a private bath, too, – a depression carved into the floor that fills from below. I do not know how this is achieved, but it delights me. A bath, in my room. Back home, clean water was a commodity. There was a rock face with a natural spring and we would go there to hold our buckets under the slow flow of ice cold water. Patience was a virtue as the trickle filled them slowly. Back home, we'd heat the water to tepid, and shiver in the chill as we bathed. But here, in this land where dragons fly the skies, there is enough hot water to fill a small pool in my bedchamber, where the floors are warm beneath my feet.

Beti bids me remove my gown and enter the pool. There are several glass vials sitting on the rim. She takes one, uncorks it and puts it beneath my nose.

"Does my lady prefer this?" she asks. The fragrance is heady. I cannot describe it. I would say it is flowers, but I have smelled too few to say for certain.

"Yes, please," I say.

"There are others, if you'd like to choose," she says, but I hold up my hand. After a life of denial, I feel the need to pace the onslaught of sensations. The kindly nurse pours only a little of the liquid into the pool and soon the entire chamber is filled with the scent.

While I enjoy my second bath since arriving, Beti leaves and returns with a wooden bowl filled with fruit and bread and hard cheeses. Zelki is right; the grapes here are as big as my hands; even the skin is sweet when I bite through it. I could not have imagined such a thing as even this single piece of fruit, but there is more. Beti slices another fruit called Thousand Sons. Inside are smaller fruits, sweet where the flesh of the surrounding mother fruit is tart. The combined flavors mingle on my tongue, delighting me. The cheeses, hard to the tooth, are smooth and creamy when chewed. The bread, brown this time, tastes a bit like nuts, and Beti confirms that indeed the flour is made from a type of nut that is ground between two giant stones in the castle mill.

She speaks of this place with pride, and when I ask her how long she has been here, she laughs and tells me she was born to service, as were her parents, her parents' parents, and so on. So many generations have served here, in fact, that her people have lost their history. She only knew that they originated in the mountains, and long, long ago, the Drakoryans enslaved and pressed them into service.

She tells me this without a hint of resentment. She is a slave, not a servant, but when I point this out, she looks at me with something of pity.

"Slaves do their duty with resentment," she says. "Slaves revolt. If there ever was resentment, it was forgotten long before my time, or my parents' time even. There has never been an uprising. "We love the Drakoryans. The greatest honor for your young sons is to join the army of the Drakoryan empire and fight alongside our masters. In the war, we fought bravely."

"There was a war?"

"Oh yes," Beti says. "Long ago. Fra'hir Castle fell under siege, as did all the castles of the Drakoryan Empire. Even King Vukurcis' castle was attacked. Those were terrible times. Terrible. It was then we lost Lord Rymoth."

"Who was the attacker?"

"Why, the enemy, of course." And then she laughs and shakes her head. "But you'll know nothing of the ShadowFell. They were driven back, and have slept now for hundreds of years."

"Wait." I sit up from where I'm reclining in the pool. "How could you remember if it was hundreds of years ago?"

She smiles. "There is much you will learn here, much of the gifts that come to those who live and serve in this realm. Had the Drakoryans not conquered my ancestors, we'd have never met, for I'd be long dead. Although we are as human as you, we've been gifted with exceptionally long lives. Not so long as the Drakoryan, mind you, but longer than you can imagine." She pauses then. "But I've said enough." She stands and reaches down for me and when I look up, I realize that I can't really read Beti's age. She could be in her thirtieth year, or her fiftieth. It's hard to tell because her face looks different depending on the angle. It's uncanny. I muse on this, pondering how my life would have been different if I'd been born on this side of the mountain. I could be with my mother, who would age slowly. I could have years and years with her. If only this gift could be extended beyond those who serve these lofty lords directly.

"Is it magic?" I think of my aunt and the other priestesses. For years, I thought I would join them, was convinced of it in my bones. My mother was almost certain of it. She used to joke that I looked like my aunt, that like Myrna, I had all the qualities of a female destined for the priesthood. Life had been so hard for my mother; her sole comfort through my childhood was her confidence that I would not fall into the clutches of the dragon.

But on the day the initiates from my year were announced, when my name did not appear in the scrying bowl, she collapsed, telling me it was an omen. I remember lifting her from the floor as I sought to comfort her. I, too, was disappointed, but told her that just because I wasn't chosen for the order did not mean the dragon would take me. There were so many girls, after all. I was but one...

She'd said nothing, and had hugged me so tightly to her chest that I could feel the beating of her heart beneath my ear.

"Why do you cry, little one?" Beti uses the pad of her thumb to wipe away the tear that has trailed down to rest on the ledge of my cheekbone, and my heart twists anew at this maternal gesture.

"Just homesick." I sniffle, feeling a a flare of renewed anger. If only my mother knew I was alive. "I envy you. You have your family."

"As will you," Beti says. "Perhaps not the one you left, but a family nonetheless. How glorious!" She towels me dry and brushes my freshly washed hair to gleaming before reaching for the blue gown and slipping it over my dead. "Think of it. Four strong mates whose devotion will be solely to you. Sons to nurture and cherish. Sisters."

"I have no sisters," I say. "I was the only child."

"The other chosen females will be your new sisters," she says firmly, and I think of Enid, how serene she seemed, how she spoke of life here with dreamlike wonder. I should be comforted, I know, but part of me remains repulsed by her acceptance, by how easily she has put aside all that should have mattered most — those who raised and loved her.

Then I think of the two men who have already roamed my body like some uncharted landscape, how they succeeded in conquering it, drawing pleasure from a reservoir I never knew existed. I think of the hands, so warm and large, roaming my curves, the long fingers that tested my virgin barrier before a mighty cock breached it, the feel of a hot tongue on places I never thought to feel a man's mouth. Even now I can feel the throbbing between my legs, unbidden but undeniable. I ponder how — when absorbing the splendor and comforts of this castle — I find my old life slipping away, supplanted by this surreal existence where fruit as large as my hand is mine for the taking, where my rags have been replaced by shimmering gowns, and my love-bruised body is replenished by dips in magical pools. It will, I realize, take a concerted effort to remember where I come from, and to fulfill my secret plan, which is to ease the suffering of my mother and aunt and the others who think I'm dead.

I am not dead. I am very much alive, and one way or another, they will know.

But I cannot think on that now. For now, I must focus on my own survival in this place, where I'm smart enough to realize that I am helpless to leave the path I've been set upon.

"You're so beautiful." Beti pivots me towards a mirror and I gaze at the woman staring back at me. It's the first glimpse I've had of myself since coming here, and the reflected image is both familiar and strange. I recognize my face as the one looking back from the small hand mirror at home. It's less pale, flushed now with a healthier glow. And my body... The dress, the fabric molding to me with a strange fluidity, glitters like a jewel. My hair cascades down my shoulders in a golden wave; when Beti asks if she can plait it. I let her, watching in the mirror as she works it into a thick braid that hangs down to my lower back.

"One more thing," she says. "Close your eyes."

I do, and feel something light settle on my skin. When I open my eyes, I realize she's tossed some sort of dust over me. It clings to my hair, my skin, reminding me of the gray silt of my village, only this is finer, and glitters, the colors changing as I move — the faintest, iridescent sheen that catches the light. Now I am a jewel, too.

Mother, if you could only see...

I don't have to wonder who knocks at the door moments later. When Zelki walks in, he stops when he sees me. The front of his leather skirt rises in carnal salute. He does not try to hide this, but smiles as he approaches me and offers me his hand.

"You are wearing my color, announcing that I have had you. When we walk into that hall, realizing every Drakoryan male knows this will fill me with pride beyond measure, for there is no fairer female in the kingdom."

"Thank you, my lord."

I drop my eyes from his. The way Zelki looks at me — I fear were I to hold his gaze a moment longer, he'd surely ravage me. I feel heat coming off his body, like some sun-warmed desert stone. Who are these strange men with dragons at their command, and why do they burn so?

The distance to the hall does not seem so long now. The celebration is still ongoing, and Zelki tells me it will continue until the final brother has claimed me. A cheer rises when we enter. Hands reach out to clap Zelki on the back. He leads me between the tables like a prize. It is a strange ritual, and I find myself wondering at the accolades. Why should they cheer a man for fucking one woman when he as fucked hundreds? Then I remember what Drorgros said, that they cheer for me, and add this to my list of things I must seek to understand.

Two brothers remain. They are seated beside Lord Drorgros, the eldest. He rises with the others to embrace Zelki with a round of congratulations. Four sets of admiring eyes are fixed on my body, and I am guided to Tythos, a broad-shouldered serious lord who does not smile, but assesses me almost coolly. I shall wear his colors next, and I find myself wondering what will happen before I don his gown.

They seat me at the table, telling me I should eat. It's another thing I must become accustomed to — the food. There is so much. This time, some sort of large birds — three, four times the size of the largest goose — sit baked to golden perfection on stone platters that line the massive tables. Each is surrounded by root vegetables drizzled with a sweet glaze. Smiling maids balance trays of breads and cakes or jugs of wine as they serve and pour. Each time one of the brothers looks away, someone raises a tankard or horn in their direction. The room is heavy with the mingled scents of food and the sounds of congratulatory cries. Tythos wordlessly piles my plate with food, explaining that the birds are a type of swan harvested from a forest pool each year for this celebration.

"Taste," he says, and like Zelki, offers me a piece from his own hand.

Will I ever tire of having my knees go weak from these new and intoxicating flavors? The moist flesh tastes like a buttery beef, the skin crunchy and almost sweet. The vegetables, which I guess to be some sort of turnip, have a mildness that magnifies the spiced sugar glaze. The flavors seem to be coordinated, like the colors of a sunset, to form a perfect culinary palette.

I could easily eat to excess, but I don't. I know what to expect now, and the nearness of the taciturn Tythos has caused a flurry of butterflies to fill my belly.

Where Drorgros wears his hair in a braid and Zelki leaves his loose, Tythos wears his in a tight bun. It accentuates his face, which is slightly more angular. His eyes are more almond-shaped than his brothers, and a darker shade of brown. His beard, while full, is more thick stubble than curls. I imagine it rubbing rough against my thighs and shift in my seat. Between my legs, my pussy is already getting wet at the thought of what awaits me with this third man. I would blame the wine for these wanton thoughts, but it remains untouched in its goblet.

After feeding me a few bites of food, Tythos turns his attention to his own food. I think of what I've experienced so far. Drorgros was gentle, instructive. Zelki was flirtatious, aggressive. Does Tythos now seek to increase my suspense by ignoring me?

I decide to ignore him, too. I turn to Imryth, who is to my right, and inquire as to the men who fill the hall. Why am I the only female, I ask?

He seems surprised that I am addressing him and glances around to Tythos, who is holding his tankard up to a maidservant coming by with a jug of wine. Of all the brothers, Imryth is the most unusual. His hair is long, but lighter, and he only has the shadow of a beard on his face. It allows me to see the line of his square jaw, the little cleft in his chin. Like the others, his is bare-chested, save for a metal-studded sash that runs around his chest, attaching to his leather skirt front to back. He is muscular, but where his brother's muscles are mounds and bulges, his are sleeker. And his eyes, greenish blue, have a depth to them, and a certain softness.

At first, he is reluctant to answer me, but finally does, telling me that the Drakoryan Empire is one big brotherhood, and aside from military victory, the one thing that binds the males above all else is this ceremony, for it celebrates the strengthening of his people with the promise of new blood, new life.

"Why take women from the villages for your mates?" I ask. "Do you not have your own women?"

"You ask many questions," he says, and unlike the dismissiveness of his brothers, there is something akin to appreciation in his tone. "I know it is difficult, not having all the answers you see." His voice is low and he leans in towards me, but I don't interpret the encroachment as flirtatious. I feel as if he's taking me into his confidence, and I like it. He turns his attention to his wine. "I am much the same."

"You understand?" I ask excitedly, perhaps more so than intended, and he glances back at me with something of bemusement in his eyes.

"My brothers chided me for it as a child. I was boundless in my curiosity, following my parents around, asking them all sorts of questions. I'd harry the servants, even my brothers, until they pushed me down. Their language is fighting..." His voice trails away.

"And yours?" I'm suddenly curious about him, but before he can answer, Tythos rises to place a huge hand on Imryth's shoulder.

"Trying to jump in line, are you, Imryth?"

I look up, piqued. "He was merely talking to me. It was pleasant, having a conversation."

Tythos stares down at me. I cannot read his expression. Is he thoughtful? Angry? Both? He takes my arm, not roughly, but with enough force to raise me to standing.

"Imryth can charm you with his words later. For now, let us take a walk."

Tythos is jealous. He has not said so, but I can feel it. There's a tension to him, and he shoots Imryth a glare before departing. I am fuming. He has no cause to be angry with his brother for not leaving me ignored. I'm wondering if I can like this man who now leads me from the hall to the sound of cheers.

He doesn't make small talk. He doesn't stop to point out or explain artwork or sculptures that line the passageway, although I long to linger and examine what looks like a shrine set up in the alcove of one wall. When I stall, he wordlessly beckons me to follow, and I do so begrudgingly.

I grow more tense, and by the time we reach the heavy door of his bedchamber, it occurs to me that I'm angry. I'm even angrier when he shuts the door and turns his back to me without a word. Tythos undoes his sash and tosses it aside. When he turns back, he makes no move to approach, but just stands there, regarding me.

"Little human," he says. "Do you have any idea how I envy your kind?"

"You? Envy us?" Whatever I expected his first words to be, they weren't this.

He smirks. "Why, yes. When your kings of old took a mate, they were not required to be faithful. They could bed their bride and go back to enjoying the bounty of other females, a different one every night, should they choose. Of course, this meant littering the land with bastards, but a Drakoryan would not have been plagued by such inconvenience. Our seed only starts to become potent when we bed our true mate. When we do, we are bound to her." He frowns. "Only her."

I stand stock still, digesting his words. "You're angry…" I can barely get the words out, nor can I hide my indignation.

"Not angry," he says, approaching. "But don't expect caresses or kind words from me. The men in the hall may cheer all they want, but tonight is no celebration for me, so if you…"

Tythos' words are stopped by the slap I land across his face, and if he is surprised, his shock is only second to mine. I have never struck anyone in my life, but I am furious with him, and can barely keep tears of rage in check as I address him.

"You're angry? I ask. *You*? You dare indulge in self-pity? *You*? Were *you* tied to a post? Were *you* plucked screaming from a ledge while your sobbing mother watched? Were *you* taken to a castle and expected to spread your legs for strangers? The only thing that has made any of this tolerable is that your brothers – to this point, anyway – gave the appearance of understanding that this was not my choice. They endeavored, at least, to talk to me, to treat me as something other than a hole to fuck."

He puts his hand to his cheek and begins rubbing it. "I've offended you."

"If you must ask," I say coldly, "then I know which brother is the slowest of wit."

This insult seems to irk Tythos in a way that the slap did not. "I could punish you for that," he says in a low, menacing tone, and I see a quick flash of yellow in his narrowing eyes. "I have a mind to put you over my lap, bare your ass, and smack you until you scream."

My heart thuds with fear at his words, but anger pounds a harder beat in my brain.

"I am *no* child," I say. "Treat me as one, and I will not submit my body. I will fight you, and while you will easily win, it will make you the only brother who had to take me by force. And I will make the others hate you for it. Mark me, Tythos."

My umbrage may have made me reckless, but my words have an instant effect. Tythos is studying me now, and I see admiration replace disdain.

"Thousands of females," he says. "They practically trip over me, eager to experience my prowess, to see if the rumors about me are true. I've had them beg me to fuck them, cry for my favor. Thousands of females, but never, ever, has one dared defy me."

"I am no whore," I say. "And I have no desire to cleave myself to you or any other man. I am doing my duty, too. If I feel an attachment, it's only because you've earned it."

"A challenge?" He smiles now, transforming his hard face into a handsome one. I see deep dimples beneath the short stubble of his beard. "I suppose we should make the best of this night, you and I."

He steps back and bows low. "Lyla, Chosen Mate of the House of Fra'hir. Will you consent to mate with me this night?"

His tone is light, but not mocking. I cross my arms, regarding him. "I don't know," I say. "Thousands of females, you say? In my village, men who shared themselves so freely suffered from diseased cocks — rashes and such."

Tythos pulls aside his skirt to expose himself. His cock is thick and veiny. I am still new to carnal delights, but instinct tells me he has every right to be proud. I think of his brothers; each wielded his cock differently. What, I wonder, will his do once inside me?

"You're welcome to inspect it more closely," he says, smiling when I blush. "It may bring you comfort to know that Drakoryans are hot-blooded, and resistant to illness. Besides, if I were carrying diseases, every maid in the hall would be on their deathbed by now."

"Is that supposed to excite me?" I ask, quirking a brow. "Knowing that I'll be another female for you to ride?"

"Oh, no," he says. "I'll not be doing the riding." He whips his skirt off, tossing it aside and walks to the bed. Unlike his brothers', his bed is made from stone, the frame carved from a solid piece rising from the floor. Across the room is the most massive fireplace I've ever seen;

what looks like an entire small tree serves as a log. There are no furs on his floor, only tightly woven straw mats. And on the walls, weapons, hung like art. Conquering. That's what he does. And I know what he wants as he lays down on his bed, his huge cock sticking straight up from a thatch of dark curls.

"Tonight, my brave little Lyla, you will ride."

I don't immediately reply. Instead, I turn, slipping the smooth fabric of my blue gown from my shoulders. It slips down, pooling at my feet. I turn, and see lust in Tythos' eyes.

I approach the bed. "I will ride you, Lord Tythos. But first, I have a question. And I know you may not answer, but it's been vexing me."

"Ask it, then," he says.

"Those dragons." I nod towards the window. "Do you ride *them*?"

"Ride them?" He puts an arm behind his head, raising himself a bit to look at me.

"Yes," I say. I move to the bed and he reaches out an arm, which I grip so he can help lift me up. "I've been told so little." I furrow my brow. "You Drakoryan control the dragons. You use them to subjugate my people, send them to fetch women like me, I presume..." I look at his face, searching his expression for affirmation, but his is unreadable. I go on. "Do you command them, or ride them?"

He looks up at the ceiling, appearing to muse on my question. "Hmm...I would think it would be dangerous to ride a dragon."

"You're teasing me," I say.

"No. I'm not. They are powerful beasts." He looks back at me. "Tell me, Lyla, if you were to ride a dragon, how would you do it? Show me. I'll not tell you another thing until you do."

The room is warm. He is laying there, his cock stiff and straight. I remember his brothers, their hands, their cocks, their tongues. My nipples harden, my pussy begins to clench. I rise to my knees.

"Well," I say. "I would think a tight grip would be essential." I swing my leg over his, straddling his huge, hard thighs, the damp curls of my pussy just grazing his skin. He tries to hide his excitement, but I feel him flinch, see his mighty cock bob. I smile. I'm learning quickly.

"A tight grip?" he says. "Dragons dip and roll. They make unexpected moves. You would need strong thighs to hold on." His gaze moves to my thighs, then between them, to my Venus mound. "Perhaps you'd need an even stronger muscle."

"Yes," I say. "One that is sure to make any beast do my bidding."

I move up. He is so large that I must rise to position myself over his cock. For a moment, I worry it will hurt to take him so soon after Zelki, but my pussy is so hot, so wet, so slick with excitement that I glide down on him, locking our bodies together. He groans.

"Just another female, right?" My voice is husky, almost unrecognizable to my own ears.

"Little tease," he says. "I should have spanked you."

I lean over, snake out a tongue to lick his nipple. It brought pleasure to me when Tythos' brother did it. Will it bring pleasure to him? He groans again, and his hands move to my ass, squeezing, and then he slaps me, the stinging pain sending a jolt of pleasure through my body. He laughs throatily. "Minx," he says. "I believe I may have underestimated you."

Tythos begins to move then. Or, at least, his cock does. He's lying on the bed, but his cock is moving up and down, pulsing up and down, softly at first, then harder. It's powerful, the length of it pulsing and receding with a rhythm that seems to change minute to minute. It snakes deeply inside of me then stops, the head of it swelling. Then the entire length of it begins to vibrate from base to tip, and I scream with a powerful internal orgasm.

And he's just getting started. His cock hardens as it vibrates. It no longer feels like flesh, but something rock hard and heavy and warm. He pulls out, turns me over and thrusts back inside me from behind. I've nearly come when he pulls out again, this time pressing the knob of his cockhead against my clit. The solid pressure vibrating against my tender nub drives me up passion's peak once more and I careen down with a wild cry. Tythos climbs from the bed and lifts me into his arms. I look down, my eyes widening in surprise. His cock has changed shape. It's hooked upward, the head a hard ball of flesh. He slides me down on it, the round bulb vibrating wildly inside me. I buck my hips against him. His lips find mine and he kisses me, laughing against my mouth. He's enjoying this, enjoying my loss of control. I tear my mouth away from his and sink my teeth into his shoulder. He cries out, grabs my ass, turns, walks to the wall where he pushes me against the stone and pounds my pussy until I can't breathe.

I reach back, grasp the thick knot of his hair, holding his head still. I look into his eyes. They are golden yellow and for a moment I feel afraid, for...no, no...surely, I'm mistaken. It's the heat, the passion, the references to riding the dragon. They're making me see things. I wrap my arms around him. He takes me back to the bed, pulls me off his cock, throws me down. I clamber to all fours, eager for more, frightened by my own wild passion, by how aroused I am by this man I thought I'd hate. My thighs are wet. I'm literally dripping both with arousal and his tribute as well. I feel a finger winding through my slit, stroking, but that can't be. There's one hand in my hair and another on my hip. It's his cock, elongated now, moving like a finger, but flattened like a tongue. It moves to my bottom hole and I cry out, reaching back. Tythos catches my wrist and I feel the tip of his cock slip just a little into my bottom hole. I cry out from the sting.

"No!" I say, and to my surprise he stops and laughs, flopping down on the bed to pull me beside him.

"One night, I will," he says.

I'm gasping, my body still heaving with the subsiding waves of my last orgasm. "One night, I'll let you."

Tythos looks at me in the fiery glow of the room.

"Little Lyla," he says. "You have amazed me this night. You have made me happy, but you have also made me feel sick with pity."

"Pity?" I ask.

"Yes. For all those females I will never fuck, all those females who will still throw themselves at me only to have me look away and say, 'No, for you cannot possibly please me as my wild little human mate does.'"

I raise myself up on one elbow. "You don't have to say that," I tell him.

"I'm not. Years ago..." He pauses. "My father told us that when the right mate came, we would want for no other. Part of me did not want to believe it. I feared it would make me less of a Drakoryan, less virile somehow. But tonight...Never have I surged like I did with you. You will be enough. The only pain will be those nights you lie with another."

I smile at him, not knowing what else to say.

And then he pulls me to him, and I sleep.

Chapter Eleven

DRORGROS

Where is Imryth?

I'm in no mood to search the castle, and bark the question at every servant I pass. I am rarely in so foul a temper. I do not like to see the servants' friendly faces transformed by fright as I snap at them, but with each shake of the head, each, "No, my lord," I grow more anxious.

Imryth is usually the reliable one. Within hours, Tythos will enter the hall with Lyla clad in ruby red, his color. The crowds will roar especially loud, for their arrival will bring the House of Fra'hir one step closer to the Deepening, and with it, the bond that quickens our seed. But the Deepening won't happen until the final mating. Imryth is the last. Where is he?

He must be in the castle, because if he isn't, that can mean only one thing — he has defied my wishes and gone to scout. I've searched it all, from the Oracle's keep to the storerooms to the pools to the libraries. I've looked in every nook and alcove. The only place I did not search was the Crystal Cavern, the exclusive realm of bonded females. It is full today with the mates of the Drakoryan celebrating in the hall. After the Deepening, Lyla will be welcomed there for her own

"I'm sure he'll return," Skryll calls after me, but I'm already allowing the change to come over me. I feel the heat rise, feel the dragon inside me start to uncoil, first as a thread of fire that courses through every vein, every artery, every available pathway. It burns me from inside, consuming my human shape. I reform as green flame, and feel the flame grow and shape itself into the semblance of a dragon. My body knits itself back together; it is the old magic at work, changing me from the Drakoryan who bedded Lyla, to the monster who burned her bonds and snatched her from the ledge. It is our secret, and one that will be revealed at the Deepening, when she will absorb the secret of our kind in the blink of an eye, when she will become one with our mystery and understand, and not be afraid.

I stand, solid now, and spread my mighty wings, thrusting myself over the inland sea and towards the dot of light that grows bigger as I approach. I burst through the cave mouth, wheeling through the air, my nostrils flaring. I search my mind, seeking to lock into Imryth's, but he has closed his to me. That was my first clue that he was not in the castle. I can feel my brothers, even when I cannot see them, and they, me. It is not a bond as strong as what we will feel with our mate, but it is still there.

I do not need to hear his thoughts to know where to go. He's patrolling, taking Bartax with him. I can appreciate his desire to scout, to look for any signs that the enemy may be closer, but today it is just too risky.

I bank to the east; he will want to check the closest villages. I increase my speed, finding an air current. I could easily drift along on it, but today I use it to enhance my speed. As I pump my wings, the landscape below becomes a blur. I slow down over a village, glancing at it through holes in the clouds. I am too high up for the villagers to see me, but with my superior sight I can hone in on them. Patches of crops spring celebration, and after that, she will become its official Mistress, hosting other human mates in the cavern whenever there is a council meeting or other affairS here at Castle Fra'hir.

There is only one place to look. I descend to the bowels of the castle, past the dungeon to a hidden passage that leads to a great cave opening to an inland sea. Here there are platforms that jut out over the water. A dragon rests on one of the rocks. I recognize him by his color — a silvery blue. It is Skryll, one of Enid's mates in his drake form. I saw him at dawn, reeling in the sky and sparring for fun with one of his brothers. I call to him now and he lifts his head and yawns, a plume of smoke rising from his throat. He sits up, stretching as we begin a telepathic communication common to our kind.

"Drorgros. What brings you here?"

"Where's your brother, Bartax?"

He stretches again, rubbing his eyes. "He left earlier, with Imryth."

I curse under my breath. "Did he say where they were going?"

"No, only that they'd be back before everyone in the hall woke up."

"Curses to those two. I told my brother not to leave!"

"He's probably just sparring," Skryll says. "I'm sure he'll be back soon. It's his night with your mate, after all. Surely…"

I turn away, not wanting to alarm Skryll. So far, we are the only ones who know about the ShadowFell. We will have to call the council soon enough, but I do not want to raise panic before the Deepening, especially given the prophecy. Once we have all consummated the union with Lyla and formed our bond, then we will call the lords together. They will want more confirmation than just the word or our oracle. This will call for a visit to the witches. There will be much to discuss.

But first things first.

"I need to find him," I say.

from the ashy surroundings. Each year we allow them a little more fertile ground, as a reward. The rest we keep burnt.

I accelerate again and there, on the horizon are two dragons, red and slate gray. I arc wide, diving below a mountain ridge and come up through a pass, dodging and weaving through the peaks.

I shoot between two mountains, surprising them. They separate, wheeling through the air, pushed apart by the gusts of my wings. Bartax recovers first, then Imryth, who hits an updraft, shoots skyward and recovers. He whirls on me in the air, roaring in indignation.

I move in front of him and roar back.

Brother, you defied me.

Brother, you are not my father.

Brother, our mate awaits. Have you forgotten?

Brother, we have enemies afoot. Have you?

We face one another, both seeking to hover in place as we beat our wings inward. It's a test of strength in which we both seek to hold our position against the competing gust.

We will discuss this at home. A growl accompanies Imryth's thought message.

Yes, we will.

He banks away, and I follow, close on his tail. I know Imryth. By the time he gets back he will retreat, not from fear, but from indignation. I do not want this. He is intense when offended. He is not like Zelki, whose heated temper burns itself out. Imryth's mood turns dark. I must talk to him, explain once again why I have fetched him back. I do not want him brooding when he goes to Lyla. The last mating is as important as the first. A good one enhances the power of the Deepening. A bad experience, or lack of connection, can create a block.

Imryth is rocketing towards home, and I push myself to catch him. When I do, I will confront him. I will fix this.

Chapter Twelve

LYLA

Tythos is gone. He left me sleeping. I awake to find Beti sitting by the huge stone bed. When I quickly pull a blanket over myself to cover my nakedness, she chuckles and asks if everyone is so modest in my village. She asks me why someone so beautiful is ashamed of her skin. I've never looked at it that way.

When I rise from the bed, I realize what a powerful lover Tythos was. I'm still tired, and more than a little sore. Unlike the others, he took me more than once, waking me at least twice. I know my nights with him will not include much sleep. Despite Imryth's kindness, the thought of lying with him fills me with dread. How can my poor body endure? Then I remember the pools and ask Beti if she can take me.

She's more than happy to, and gives me a shift to wear until I change into Tythos' gown. The cheering, she assures me authoritatively, will be thunderous when I am handed off to the last brother. She chats merrily as we walk, describing the food and merriment I can expect at the final nights of the celebration, how grand it will be. I try to listen, but all I can think of is sinking into the healing waters.

I'm lucky, she says, to get to enjoy the pools in private. Before the other lords leave to return to their own castles, this cavern will be filled with Drakoryans replenishing themselves after days of drinking and feasting. I'm glad, too. I'm in no mood to see anyone now, although when she mentions food, my stomach growls. To my embarrassment, Beti hears it.

"You're hungry," she observes, looking around, and frowns. "Meda is supposed to keep a bowl of fruit here. That lax girl. When I see her, I shall box her ears. Would you like me to fetch some?"

"Would you?" I ask, my stomach growling again as I think of the huge grapes and juicy melons I've come to crave.

"Yes." But then looks worried. "Maybe I shouldn't go. I can't let you stay in too long."

"Don't worry. I won't," I promise. "Zelki warned me. Only a few moments, until I feel less tired and sore. I'm starving. Please?"

Beti hovers a moment more, but when I assure her I'll be fine, she scurries off. I climb into the pool, finding a ledge where I can sit and sink up to my neck. The relief is instant. I feel the fatigue lift from my body. My sore nipples and pussy tingle as the tenderness dissipates. I lean back and close my eyes.

Just a moment, I tell myself, but a moment turns into two, and then more. The feeling is intoxicating. I hear a dripping sound and open my eyes, looking for the sound that seems to come just to my left, but there is nothing. I sit up, searching, for it is getting louder. I find myself focusing on a stalactite on the far side of the massive cavern, and when I do, I gasp. Even though it is far across the cavern, I am seeing with great clarity. And the small drop of water dripping from the end of it makes the sound I heard. That, too, is magnified.

I climb from the pool, cursing myself. I promised Beti I'd be careful, and I wasn't. I wonder how long the effect will last. Hopefully not long. Zelki was right. My senses feel overwhelmed.

I don my shift I was wearing when I entered, letting it slip over my still wet body. It clings to my skin. I undo the plait of hair I'd bundled on top of my head and let it fall. I feel restless and begin to walk around, hoping to expend some of the energy that sits like a ball in my belly. I meander between the pools until I reach a wall. I wonder if it is warm. I reach out to touch it, and when I do, I instantly draw back in fright.

Did I cause the noise I heard? It's not a dripping this time, but something else, something loud. I touch the wall again, and hear nothing, at least not at first. But a moment later, there it is again. A roar. And a whooshing noise.

Dragons. I can hear them. I can hear them through the walls. My heart begins to pound as my mind flashes back to the moment I saw the massive head, that huge, knowing eye. The dragon was a beast I should never have wanted to see again. The mere notion should scare me. Why am I so driven to see them? Is it because the Drakoryan are hiding them from me? They say all will be revealed if I will only wait. I do not want to wait.

They are close. I have to see them. I rush from the cavern, tilting my head to discern the direction of the sound. It's to the right, and down. I break into a run, drawn by the noise I can still hear. The cavern narrows and grows darker. I stop long enough to wrench a candle from one of the sconces before hastening onward.

Why is it taking so long? I'm not tired, but I am baffled. I can hear movement of something large ahead. Then it occurs to me. The pool. What I'm hearing is still far off. I should stop. I should return to the pool. Beti will be in such a state, and no doubt feel betrayed by my departure. But my curiosity burns in me. Zelki only allowed me a glimpse. There is a dragon down here, and I am determined to see it all, and up close.

Think of the danger!

My sensible mind tries to reason with my overwhelming willfulness. But I am energized, propelled by this singular desire. I continue to run, and then I hear pounding and ahead, I see dim light. There is an opening. I sprint faster, not tiring even though my lungs are burning.

I force myself to slow, however, as I reach the end of the tunnel. I see water. Lots of it. At the end of the tunnel is a huge, flat rock. Beyond that is more water than I've ever seen in my life. It slams against the edge of the flat rock, throwing up salty spray and foam. The water is hemmed in by a massive cave lit by small openings in the rocks overhead. Ledges stick out from the rocks, and there, on one of them, is a silver blue dragon. Another, steel gray, wheels above and settles on a far ledge, roaring. The silver dragon answers. I cover my ears. The sound is so loud I feel as if my head my split, but I do not leave. I train my eyes on it, availing myself of my keen senses to focus. I put my hand to my mouth, stifling a cry of delight.

It's real, and beautiful, with silvery blue scales. It is resting now, its eye closed tight, its serpentine neck curled around its body, its wings folded along its back. Is this where they keep them, then? Do the Drakoryan lure them in? I look around for food, for what else would entice these beasts to rest in this subterranean cavern. Does the water draw them? Can they swim? How did the Drakoryan come to master these huge creatures, to get them to do their bidding? I have so many questions, but another sound has gotten my attention. Another roar, and the sound of it reverberates through my body even though I cannot see its source. The dragons hear it, too, and raise their heads. I duck behind a pillar, turning my focus towards the mouth of the cave. I hear the roar again, and then another.

A winged shape appears. Another dragon. No, *two* dragons! One is chasing the other, and when they move beneath the shaft of light coming through the top of the cave, I can see the color of the first one. It's gold. And then I see the second one, larger and fierce. Green. And I know with one glance that this isn't just any dragon. This is *my* dragon, the one that snatched me from the ledge. It's chasing the gold one, which dips and dives. The green one seeks to intercept it, spreading its wings, but the gold dragon is too fast. It shoots upward, looping over and past the green dragon, and I realize with horror that they are now both coming right for this ledge, right for me!

Even though I'm behind the ledge, the force of the wind from the gold dragon's wings as it brakes nearly knocks me down, and the ground vibrates under my feet as it lands heavily on the ledge. The green dragon is next, and I sink down to keep from falling, gripping the pillar as I peek from behind it. The dragons are facing one another. The green one circles the golden one, curving its body around it as if trying to contain it. The gold one flattens its neck and roars a warning and I hold my ears, the sound so loud as to be painful.

What happens next should make me scream, but the shock of it freezes my voice in my throat. The gold dragon backs up and instantly bursts into flame. The green dragon does the same and I stare, hand over my mouth at these twin towers of fire – one green, one gold - where two dragons had just been. The flames begin to condense, shrink and take on another shape. The shape of men. And then, before my eyes, the flaming men solidify, and there before me stand two Lords of Fra'hir, the one who took my virginity, and the one who is supposed to bed me tonight.

And now I find my voice. And I scream.

Chapter Thirteen

DRORGROS

Lyla. What is she doing here? Suddenly nothing else matters, not my anger at my brother, not my desire to keep him from fleeing before we can sort out our differences.

Why did she come here? Even that doesn't matter. Because she is here. Her keening scream entered my human ears as I shifted, getting my attention. It's gotten my brother's too. When I turn to him, I see my worry reflected in his eyes.

"Lyla." He is the first to speak and moves towards her, but she's shaking her head. She tries to take a step back, but the shock of what she's seen has locked her legs. She falls backwards to sitting on the ground, staring up at us.

"No," she says, and begins to cry. "No. No. No."

"Lyla." I keep my voice gentle as I walk to her. Her chest is heaving through her thin shift, her breasts visible beneath the sheer white fabric. Behind her is a spent candle. She's come through the tunnels. I channel the anger I feel towards Beti. She was supposed to be minding Lyla. What happened? But that is not important now, either. My brother and I flank her, kneel.

"Lyla..."

"You!" She looks wildly from one face to the other, scooting backwards and raising herself to standing. She looks wildly at Imryth, then at me. "You don't *command* dragons. You *are* dragons!" She begins to sob, her tears unbidden. "It was you who took me from the ledge. It was you who burned my village!" She launches herself at me, her fists pounding wildly on my chest. I'd be amused if her pain weren't so palpable. I glance at Imryth and then pick Lyla up, restraining her in my arms. My mind flashes back to the day I took her from the ledge, how warm she felt in my grasp as I lifted her high into the air. She fought until she lost consciousness in the thin atmosphere. She fights now, but does not stop. She is cursing at me, scratching as we make our way through the tunnel.

I move quickly, praying we don't encounter another Drakoryan taking a break from the hall to spread his wings before resting on one of the ledges. As it is, Skryll and Bartax have no doubt seen and heard more than they should have. I remind myself to send someone to speak with them.

By the time we reach Lyla's bedchamber, she has given up her futile attempts to extricate herself from my arms. She has fallen silent, having run out of names to call me. I enter her room with Imryth on my heels. Beti is there, and her apology dies in her throat when she sees my expression. I glare down at her.

"Out," I say. She flees and Imryth shuts the door behind her. I place Lyla on the bed. I expect her to curl up into a ball and weep, but she rises instead and walks to the tiny window of her room. She may have spent her rage in my arms, but she is still seething. My brother and I remain silent as she collects herself. When she turns, there are tears coursing down her cheeks, and her lip trembles in anger as she speaks.

"You could have told me," she said. "You could have given me the choice."

"And have you judge us by our dragon form alone?"

"Better a form that burns than one that deceives. Both your forms steal and destroy. You stole my innocence, Lord Drorgros, with your betrayal. You have destroyed my trust with your secrets."

What can I say to this? I have no words, but Imryth does. "You have every right to be angry," he says. "You have every right to hate us.'"

"Brother," I begin, but he holds up his hand, silencing me as he makes his way over to Lyla.

"Ours is an ancient race, set in our ways, adherents to tradition. We are Drakoryan — half man, half dragon. We walk between the worlds of land and sky, forever restless. If we fail to put our trust in you enough to give you the truth, please understand it's because we — more than anyone — know how hard it is to trust a dragon. How can you trust something that rules through destruction? Here is a secret for you, Lyla: In human form, we fear the dragon that lurks inside. We are forever cursed with the task of controlling it. We understand the primal fear of dragons, even as we have embraced it as the other side of our nature, even as we revel in the power of becoming one. There is beauty in dragons, and loyalty, but to trust one, you must first know its heart, its thoughts. As Drakoryans, our human form allows us to give a voice to the beast. We keep the secret from our human mates until we have all known her, touched her, convinced she is ours, and we are hers – loyal to the death."

"Who made you?" she demands to know, and Imryth smiles and touches her face.

"That, my dear, is a story forged over ages, and a story that would take ages to tell. Of course, our history has been written, and if you can forgive us for deceiving you, if you can accept us..." He kneels now, taking Lyla's hand. "You will know our history. You will know all." He puts her hand to his forehead. "Please, despite what you see, despite what monsters you think us to be, give us a chance. Please. Be our mate. Please. Forgive us."

I stand in silence, marveling at the image before me. Lyla, so small, so innocent in her shift, her naked body visible through the fabric. My brother, so large, but kneeling to place her hand on his head as if he were her pet, her servant.

"Do I have a choice?" she asks.

Imryth takes her hand, puts the palm to his mouth and kisses it gently before clasping it between his. I hold my breath. "I would not take you without your consent," he says. "I would endure the wrath of my kin, my brothers, the inner beast, before I would force you."

Everything rests on her now. My eyes are focused on my quiet brother, who has just placed the entire fate of House Fra'hir in one tiny human's hands.

Lyla is unreadable as she stares down at my kneeling brother. I am rooted to the floor, as afraid now as she was in the cave. I know Imryth. He does not bluff. If she says no, he will not take her. If he does not take her, there will be no Deepening, no mating. Our line will end. He is giving this little human all the power, all the control.

"If I consent, I'll have your sons?" she asks.

"If you consent, come mating time, yes," he replies.

Worry clouds her pretty face. "You're half dragon," she muses. "I do not desire to have a baby dragon, or to...lay an egg."

I cannot help but laugh now, and even Imryth is smiling. "No, little one. You will have a son as fine and fair as you. Drakoryan do not assume their dragon form until their thirteenth season. I promise you, our sons will be as human as you until they are nearly men. No doubt, they will test you nonetheless, especially if they inherit their mother's curiosity."

She looks at me. She looks at Imryth.

"And if I refuse? Will I go home?"

"No," Imryth answers honestly. "You will live in exile here, in one of the villages. You will be cared for, but your wishes will be respected. You will remain untouched until the end of your days."

"Untouched..." Lyla puts her free hand to her chest. "Untouched." She whispers the word. She falls silent then, staring towards the window, then moves the hand from her breast to my brother's head.

We wait for her to speak. She is thinking. I can tell she thinks a lot. I want to rush to her, to shake her, to demand an answer. I am afraid. But I must trust her as I ask her to trust us. Finally, she speaks.

"I have made my decision," she says. "I never thought to leave my home. I had prayed in the night not to be taken by the dragon. But I was. It cannot be for nothing. What I have been through, cannot have been for nothing. All of this...it has touched me beyond the physical. It touches my head, my heart. Even when I am angry, I long to know more, to walk this path I thought to resist." She pauses. "I will accept you, Imryth, Lord of Fra'hir, as I accepted your brothers. And I will accept what follows as my fate."

If I could shout a cheer, I would. But I restrain myself, as does Imryth, who only kisses her hand as he rises.

"Thank you," he says. "Now, with reluctance, I will return you to Tythos, who will give you his gown. I will see you tonight, in the hall." He bows. "Until then."

He leaves, and I offer Lyla my arm. We do not speak as we walk back to Tythos' chamber. The woman beside me, while small, walks taller, and with more confidence. I am impressed, intrigued. We could not have picked a better mate.

Chapter Fourteen

LYLA

Tythos had swelled with pride as we entered the hall. I feel like a living flame now, dressed in his color. I know now that the gowns represent the color of their dragon forms. Drorgros is green, Zelki is blue, Tythos, red. The last gown I wear shall be gold, Imryth's color.

He smiled almost shyly as Tythos reluctantly handed me off amid the thunderous roar from the crowd. My hearing was still sensitive from my time in the pool. The noise made my head pound, but I allowed myself to absorb the excitement and optimism in the room, and unlike previous times, this time I turned to the crowds and flashed a brief smile. They roared louder.

The wine had been even more plentiful and sweeter, the feast more lavish. Massive pigs, their mouths stuffed with apples the size of melons, were placed on the tables by male servants who groaned under the weight of the platters. The sight of the beasts, whose eyes had been replaced with golden fruit, was unnerving. But the meat was tender and mild and salty-sweet, the skin crisp and juicy and flavorful. There were huge tureens of soup. I grew tired of asking what kinds they held. Some were spicy, some savory. I could only sample a little of each for the richness of them. There were huge mushrooms swimming in wine sauce, long loaves of bread filled with soft, unborn grains, cakes and pies with juices that bubbled from beneath golden crusts.

I understood, now, the Drakoryan appetites and why, despite all the food, each plate and platter was cleaned by the time we left. They are, after all, half dragons.

And now, here we stand, in Imryth's chamber. It is as different from the other chambers as he is from his brothers. It could be a wizard's lair, this Drakoryan's chamber. It is the only one with books, and there's a long table under the leaded window covered in scrolls and maps and sketches and curious creations half-finished - wooden creatures operated with tiny cogs and levers.

There's a huge dragon scale in the corner. Imryth has fashioned it into a shield. The front is engraved with the silhouette of a dragon head, the style simplistic but elegant. When I admire it, he lifts it and places the leather bands on the inside over my arm.

"You're a warrior now," he says. The shield is solid, and hard, but lighter than I would have imagined.

"It's so beautiful," I say.

"It's yours."

I look up at him. "No." I slip it off my arm. "I couldn't."

"You can. And you will. Anything I have is yours now, Lyla. Look around the room. I love the way you examine everything. It makes me want to share it with you. Besides, watching you has given me the time I need."

"Time for what?" I ask.

He falls silent, then smiles an almost boyish smile. "Time to figure out how to seduce you."

I slip the shield off my arm and gently set it down before looking up at him. My face is flushed.

"I've never been seduced," I say.

He chuckles. "Given that your experience is limited to my brothers, I don't doubt it. But don't take that as an insult to them. They are unrestrained in their passion. They demand it in return. I would draw it from you, Lyla."

He hasn't even touched my body, but the way his words touch my mind has evoked a physical response that's just as strong. My nipples tighten against the red gown. My pussy pulses softly. I'm already wet.

He takes my hand and begins to speak, his voice deep and soft:

"A maiden stood upon a rock,

A dragon came to call.

He plucked her up into the air

She fought but did not fall

A Lord unto that maiden came

And plucked her flower fair

His brother came and then another

Each took her to his lair

She wore their gowns – green, blue and red -

Until at last she stands

In my chamber, not filled with dread

With my heart in her hands."

I am speechless. The rise and fall of his love poem is beautiful.

"Did you write that?" I ask.

"No," Imryth says. "It just came to me. Would you like me to write it down for you?"

I nod.

"Would a lady mind if I did it later? It pleases me to look at you, Lyla. I do not want to look away." He smiles. "I don't think I can, really." His finger is tracing the fabric running across the shoulder of my gown. "May I?" he asks.

I nod. He slips the fabric off my shoulder and reaches for the other side. "May I?"

"Please," I say.

Can he feel my excitement? It rushes through me in waves. I look at his fingers as he gently slides the gown off my shoulders. His long fingers. They've fashioned delicate drawings, made wondrous little articulated devices. But all I can think about now is having those fingers thrust into my aching pussy, or having the mouth that recited such sweet poetry capturing my nipple with heated pressure.

"I've flown thousands upon thousands of miles," Imryth says when the gown falls. "I've seen towering mountains backlit by glorious sunsets, blazing comets that lit up the night sky. I have seen waterfalls that start in cloud-shrouded peaks and end in explosions of mist miles below. I've seen vast deserts, whole seas of shifting sand. I've seen oceans that never seem to end. I have seen all these things and more, Lyla. But I have never seen anything more beautiful than the woman standing before me."

Another feeling has joined the warmth of arousal. It's a different kind of warmth that floods through my chest and makes me weak in the knees. When Imryth lowers his mouth to mine, I stand on my tiptoes to meet his lips, parting them to allow his tongue. His mouth is warm; his tongue swoops over mine, nimble as a dragon, and as bold. My gentle poet is taking control of me, and I abandon myself to him, allowing this final brother to scoop me from the floor and take me to his bed. His bed. There are no posts, no heavy canopy. Imryth has painted constellations on the ceiling. I spread my legs and arms for him under the stars and he descends, his powerful body molding to mine. He whispers in my ear as he winds my hand in his hair. I run my hands down his back, tracing his muscles, his spine. I find the clasp of his leather sash and unhook it. He kisses me as he pulls it aside and I laugh against his mouth as both our hands meet trying to remove his leather skirt.

He traps my hand then, guiding it to his cock. I lift myself and look down. Like the rest of him, it is lean and sleek, the narrow, arrow-like head positioned now just between my legs. Imryth slides into me with a satisfying thrust and dips his head towards my breast to capture my nipple in his mouth. I arch off the bed, my legs tight around his waist. And when he's completely embedded in me, I feel a small nudge against my clitoris, like a finger. But his hands have trapped mine above my head, pinning them down. He's looking into my eyes, gauging the wonder as I discover his special talent. His cock is deep within me, but there is something else flick, flick, flicking away at my clitoris. It moves with the same kind of dexterity as Tythos' cock, only...it can't be...

"Such a passionate lady deserves more than one," he whispers with a wink and I reach my hand down.

"If need be," he says as I marvel at what I'm feeling, "I can bring double the pleasure to my beautiful mate."

He begins to pound me then, driving me up and back on his mattress until my toes curl with ecstasy and I scream my orgasmic pleasure up to the painted stars. I'm still coming when he turns me over. And now I feel one cock seeking my pussy as a second emerges and probes at the crinkle of my bottom hole. This time I look back. I want to see, even though I'm afraid. And it's oddly natural, even though I know it is not. He can change the size and shape of both cocks; they are long and thin now, and both gently pushing into me. My pussy is clenching around one as I gasp against the sting of the second entering my bottom. Both are just the width of a finger, but then the first — fully embedded now — begins to swell and pulse. The second, narrow still, continues to slide in. The feeling of fullness is arousing me beyond measure. I feel thoroughly taken, impaled as I am by this most unusual of lovers. And now the second cock begins to expand, and I moan as he begins to move, stroking me from the inside as his fingers find my clit, rubbing it in slow circles as I writhe and moan into the bedcovers.

He probes me from the inside, exploring, stroking. He brings me to the edge of orgasm and pulls back, laughing when I mewl in frustration. And when I finally beg to come, he drives me hard, the softness gone as he pushes me through a string of climaxes so powerful that I can't catch my breath. Imryth has made an art of sex, wringing pleasure from my body until I think I can take no more. And then, he shows me I can, whispering words of love in my ear as he rises with me on one final wave that culminates with a dual explosion of his seed.

"You are mine, now," he says when he finally withdraws. He holds me gently in his arms, stroking my face as I play with his hair. "Mine, and Drorgros' and Tythos' and Zelki's. We have joined with your body, my brothers and me. But tomorrow, we will join with you here, where it counts the most." He touches my temple, then kisses it. "And then, you will fully be our mate."

Chapter Fifteen

DRORGROS

"Are they going to lock themselves away all day?" Zelki grumbles as he holds his horn out for more wine. Normally, I don't care how much he drinks, but I put my hand over the opening before the maid can fill it a fourth time.

"You've had enough, brother. Drink and brooding don't mix. And are we to begrudge Imryth his mating time? He waited for us."

"He lost to us in combat, remember?" Zelki says, snatching the horn away from me.

"I envy him in a way," Tythos says. "He gets to enjoy her at his leisure."

"Listen to you two, mooning about." I can't help but shake my head. "It's not as if we won't have her again. The fun is just beginning, after all. She knows us now, has been fully inducted into the mysteries of the flesh. When we next take her, it will be after the Deepening. Lovemaking will have reached a new dimension."

I speak with confidence, but I am only going on what I have been told. In truth, I am as eager as they to experience this next level of interaction with our mate. And although I don't show it, I am just as eager to see her walk through the door.

There is always a level of competitiveness between Drakoryan siblings once they take a mate. The adjustment period is hard. Among the sons of Rymoth, there is already something of a balancing act between us now that our father is gone. Our father was always the peacemaker. Now we add sharing a mate to the sharing of power in House Fra'hir. With the looming threat of the ShadowFell, we must work hard to remain united.

The hall tonight is filled to capacity, not just with Drakoryans, but with their mates. My gaze travels through the room, falling here and there on human women surrounded by their protective and doting males. There's placid Enid, who arrived terrified but quickly took to her Bartax, Skryll, and Oxyl of House Gro'han. They will breed this Mating Time and for the next three years she will bear sons. There's Kya, who was initially so grief-stricken for home that she cut off her hair in protest. Her mates, Zorin, Amul, and Jiln of House Bri'ja, feared they'd never reach her, and it took much longer than average to bring her along. Still, their Deepening, when it happened, was powerful, and their love is evident even now as the trio surround the laughing human with short red curls.

It takes more than plucking a human maiden from the ledge to make her a mate. It is not always easy, and after the Deepening, Lyla will join a sisterhood of females who will help her better understand her new life. But that is yet to unfold. I turn my attention from the future to the present as the massive doors open. The cheers would shake the halls of a lesser castle, and I smile to see Imryth enter with Lyla on his arm. She is so resplendent in my brother's golden color that I feel a catch in my throat. I begin to cheer, too, and look over at my brothers. Tythos raises his voice. Zelki, too, is cheering, having put aside his jealousy to show his solidarity.

Lyla's eyes widen as she realizes there are other females here. I see her happy recognition as she sees others from her village, women like Enid whom she had assumed dead. They rush forward to embrace her briefly before she is swept farther down the narrow passage that has opened in the crushing crowd of celebrants. My other brothers and I wait patiently. The men clap Imryth on the back as the women continue to push towards Lyla, clasping her face and covering it with kisses. She is overwhelmed, crying one moment and laughing the next. Imryth looks as happy as I've ever seen him.

"It seems our scholarly brother has found something more interesting than a dusty book," Tythos says with a laugh, and I join him. When our brother reaches us, we embrace him and surround Lyla, shutting her off from the crowd, which falls back to returns to their seats. Not everyone will get a chance to greet the couple, but there are hundreds of years to get acquainted.

As we take our places at the table, Lyla turns to me. "I never thought to see this much food in all the world, let alone in one place."

I chuckle, understanding her amazement. Tonight's feast is impressive, even by our high standards. Whole sides of beef, boar stuffed with fruit, baked pheasants piled as if they were quail, drumsticks half as long and wide as a man's arm. There are double the tureens of soup, bowls piled with freshly harvested greens and mushrooms, some cooked, some raw, and every kind of fruit that grows in the empire. And tonight, more desserts than even I have ever seen. Puddings, boiled and baked, send plumes of sweet-scented smoke wafting over the tables. Towers of pastries tumble as hands pluck one or two from the base, sending them rolling around massive pies bursting with hot berry filling.

And finally, there is wine. We have saved our best for this night, so sweet and potent that a few glasses have the room bursting into songs of our forefathers, songs of celebration containing lyrics in the ancient tongue, drake-song.

Lyla watches me and my brothers as we sing. I see her mouth trying to form the words she hears. It is a beautiful sight, our quick-witted mate seeking to understand.

Soon, I want to tell her, *you will*. Tomorrow, after the feast, you will know.

But tonight, we eat. We make merry. We celebrate our union with the woman who will bear sons that carry on the legacy of House Fra'hir.

Chapter Sixteen

LYLA

It is time.

It is the day of the Deepening, and I do not know what to expect.

For the first night since arriving in House Fra'hir, I slept alone in my bedchamber, where I was taken after the feast.

When I wake, Beti is waiting. I instantly try to apologize for leaving the pools, but she brushes me aside. A lady, she says, does not apologize to a servant. I am a Drakoryan mate now, she tells me, and part of my role is to remember my place, as she will remember hers.

She is not resentful, and as the day wears on, is good company. She brings me breakfast – an egg as large as my hand, its butter-yellow yolk rich and delicious, bread, and a slab of some kind of dried meat brined in a flavorful salt. This is served with stewed apples scented with spices, and a cup of creamy milk.

She fills the bath in my room, scenting the water with fragrant oils. She insists on bathing me, and I relax under her hands and think of my mother. Mother – whose memory keeps me from being fully happy. She remains behind in the village where I grew up watching the skies for the monsters we were told to fear, monsters who allowed us only so much productive ground while turning the rest to ash as they sped over, raining pillars of fire from above. Why did the Drakoryans never come to us in human form? Why did they only show themselves as the thing that would terrify us the most? Why have they left so many families to mourn, rather than giving them cause to celebrate? Mother. I think she would be sad, still, to lose me, but happy to know that I am alive and cared for and pampered.

I live in a castle, Mother. A castle. A tear comes to my eye. I wish I could send her my thoughts, but even if that were possible I doubt they could penetrate the thick walls of this castle fortress. I force myself to look ahead, instead of looking back, at least for now.

Beti has helped me from the bath. She will dress me today, she says, and goes to a huge wardrobe, where she fetches a gown that takes my breath away. I can barely speak as she slips it over my head and I turn to face the looking glass. The gown shimmers with the combined colors of my Drakoryan mates, changing color depending on how I move. It is cut low, showing the swell of my breasts. My hair will be worn loose today, with no adornment save for a gold circlet inlaid with tiny jewels of red, green, and blue.

"Are you ready?" Beti asks. I've been staring at myself for some time now, not from vanity, but from wonder. I see myself now as they see me – Drorgros, Zelki, Tythos, and Imryth. I see myself as a woman. Their woman.

"I am ready," I respond, although I'm not sure what awaits. No one has explained the Deepening. No one has told me what it entails other than it will increase my understanding of my new life, of my role here.

Drorgros comes for me. When he walks in, he stops and stares.

"Is something wrong, my lord?" I ask.

"No," he says. "Nothing at all. You are perfect." He holds out his arm. I take it. He guides me from the room, down a stair. We take another passageway this time, one I have not seen. Finally, we come to a heavy door. It opens to a surprisingly nondescript, windowless room with dark stone walls. The only lighting is a stand holding six pillar candles. There is a single chair in the center of the room. A hooded figure stands beside it. As I approach, he lifts his head and removes the hood. His hair is whiter than white, his beard long and tied near the bottom by a beaded cord.

"Lyla of Fra'hir, cherished mate of the sons of Rymoth." He looks me in the eye. His are small pinpricks of blue peering from under the bushy caterpillars of his brow. But they are timeless and knowing. "Are you ready to take your final step? Are you ready for the Deepening?"

I weigh my answer. "I do not know," I say. "What is required?"

"An open mind and a brave heart." He smiles, transforming his stern face into grandfatherly kindness. "You have both, I think."

"What will I receive?"

"Ah," he replies, nodding in approval. "Outspoken enough to ask what *you* will benefit. Not all females are so bold. I can see why the Wyrd chose you."

"Wyrd?"

Another enigmatic smile. He does not address my second question, but does answer my first. "You will benefit by gaining what you seek. Knowledge — the foundational understanding required to survive and thrive in our world." He raises a bushy brow. "Perhaps, if prophecy holds true, to lead as no female has before."

I look at the brothers. They are listening, but do not interrupt. Whoever this old man is, he has their respect. I look back at him. I listen to my heart.

Am I ready? I ask it.

You are ready, it says.

Did the old man hear my silent exchange? He nods as if he did and moves aside, gesturing to the chair. I sit and the brothers approach, each laying their hands on me. Their hands are warm, warmer than usual. When I look up, their eyes have changed to golden, the pupils elliptical. I've seen this change in flashes of passion, but it is holding now, and they seem to be falling into some sort of trance. The old man pulls a book from his robes and begins to read.

I do not understand the language. The words are heavy with conso-nants. The vowels sound like wind. It is the sound of metal on metal, the sound of a forge. The language of fire. That is my last thought before I feel myself pulled backward, down, into a tunnel. I am falling. I open my mouth to scream, but nothing comes out. I hit something soft, and am squeezed into a tiny space. I open my eyes. I open my mouth. What emerges is an infant's wail.

I am in the body of a baby. I train my eyes downward, seeing a cord on my belly leading between the open and bloody thighs of a woman. Hands lift me and lay me on her breast.

"A son! A son!" I hear a cry from far away. I struggle to focus on the mother whose voice I recognize. She has dark hair. She puts a breast to my mouth. I root around instinctively, my tiny face pushing against the mound of flesh as I seek the nub of a nipple.

"Welcome, Drorgros, firstborn of Rymoth," she says wearily.

As I swallow her first milk, my body pinwheels and spirals out of the infant. I am zooming backward, then forward. I fall, hitting the ground. I do not taste milk in my mouth now. Instead, I taste blood.

"Get up! Get up!" A boot is jabbing my side. There is red dirt in my eyes. It stings. I sputter and cough, trying to blink back tears. I cannot cry. Not now. I stagger to my feet and before I can find my balance, a sword hilt is pressed into my palm. Strong hands grip my shoulders and spin me around. I am facing a tall youth. He is blonde, with a confident smile. He clutches a sword and a shield fashioned from dragon scale.

"You left yourself open, Tythos! That's why Bartax took you down. Try again."

"Why?" I look up. I know the man I see through these eyes is Rymoth, my father. "Why should I learn to use a sword when one day I will be a mighty dragon?"

My father laughs. "Because a man form is easier to kill. And a man form must learn to fight, lest his enemies wait until he is weakest." He shoves me forward. "Fight! Think like a warrior!"

I raise my sword. Bartax, taller and quicker, comes at me again. I am ready this time. I think like a warrior. I think like my father. I dodge, I duck, I strike. Bartax falls.

I shoot straight up and am in darkness again. I am drifting in darkness. I am above the castle. Birds wheel and cry around me. I drop, zooming down into darkness. I hit something warm. I am in yet another body.

I am in an alcove, in the body of a little boy. I am crying. Mother is there. "Imryth," she says. "Imryth. Why does my brilliant son weep?" She rests my head on her belly. I feel my unborn brother moving there, under my cheek. She miscarried the son that was supposed to be born after me, but this year was finally strong enough to accept my father's seed at mating time. He wants five sons, she says, and she wants to give him five sons, despite the warnings of the Wyrd. Still I worry about her, and do not want to vex her further. Not when she is so tired and heavy with child.

"Nothing," I say.

"No, my dear. It is not *nothing*." She rubs my back. "Tell me, darling." Her kindness draws the truth from me.

I am not warlike, I tell her miserably. I am not a fighter. I fear that I will not have the strength to become dragon. She laughs at this. She tells me being a dragon requires more than physical strength. She tells me they are among the wisest of all creatures, able to both soar above the clouds or hide themselves in the bowels of the earth. They are the most patient, she says. When threatened with extinction, they are smart enough to know when to withdraw, and can sleep for centuries until something in them senses their fortunes have shifted. Then they wake, and rise to victory. She asks me to write her a poem about dragons. She loves my poetry, and asks me if I want to hear a secret. Yes, I say, and she leans down, whispering that of all her sons, I am the most like her. She hugs me. She is warm. I curl against her, pressing my cheek against the swell of her belly. From inside her womb, my unborn brother tries to push me away but cannot.

I am pulled away. It is very dark now, very dark. I am shooting through a dark, tight place. It hurts. I can barely emerge, and when I finally do, it is to sobs and wails. I breathe deep, exhaling a cry that joins theirs. My bloody little fists are balled. I am born furious. The cries of joyous welcome are absent. I am born into a pool of blood that soaks the bed beneath my infant body. I long for the warmth of my mother's body, to hear her sweet voice unmuffled by the womb waters. Instead, I hear a deep voice as I am bundled up.

"No! No! No! It cannot be!" My father. He is wailing the words.

"She is dying, Lord Rymoth," a nursemaid says. "There is nothing we can do."

"I will not accept it! We will take her to the Wyrd. To the pool. We will bring her back!"

"No." My mother's voice is weak. "Do...not...make me...a...wraith. That...is...not...living.."

There is more wailing. I turn my head to the sound of my mother's weak voice, but it is silent. I am unswaddled and bathed. I scream and scream. I want milk. I want my mother. My mother is dead. I am the last son of Rymoth.

"What is his name?" the attendant asks.

"Zelki," my father says.

"Do you want to hold him?"

"No. Not yet." My father leaves. I am newly born. I am angry.

I hear a moaning. It is my voice. I am trying to claw my way back to consciousness. I know now what the Deepening is. I am in the minds of my mates, feeling what made them. It is painful. I do not want to do this. But I fall back, swirling. I squeeze my eyes tight. I am fractured, splitting into three – the three oldest brothers. I am seeing simultaneously through three sets of eyes. We are on a high cliff.

It is time. There is pressure in our chests, pressure under our skin, pressure in our veins. We have been living with this pain for a month now. We have been bellowing and pacing, fighting and refusing food. Our hands burn everything we touch. We have been confined to a cave in the mountains, the only place that is safe for a Drakoryan on the cusp of the first change. This is the time when we are most dangerous. We are neither man nor dragon. We are wild creatures, and for ten days we have been chained in the cave behind us. Our father comes to let us loose. His bond to us has told him it is time.

Drorgros is ready. He is eager to make father proud. Tythos is ready. He is eager to prove himself. Imryth is ready. He is curious to see what it is to fly. Zelki is not here. He waits at home. I feel him, but not as I feel the others. He is angry to be the youngest, angry not to be ready to change.

Our father says a magic word. The heat rises through our skin. We scream. "We are burning, father! We are burning!

"Wait," he says. "Wait."

We grow as flame, mold, cool. We spread our wings, rejoicing. We are dragons. We fly.

I am seeing the world from above, the clouds, the mountain tops. I do not want this memory to end. It does.

I am sucked back through the void.

I pinwheel through the void until I thump through a stop. I am looking out through narrowed eyes, older now.

"You killed mother!" Tythos is angry with me. The argument was over something silly, some young man's bickering blown out of proportion. I can see that my brother instantly regrets his words, but it is too late. I am angry. It has been two moons since I changed, several years after my brothers. But I can change faster than they can, and I will make my brother pay for what he's said. I loved my mother. Even if I only heard her weak voice once, I know I loved her. I did not kill her. It was not my fault, being born.

I burst into towering flame, changing before my brother can even quicken. I draw back my head, feel the fire building in my throat. I will punish him. The acrid fumes await ignition.

"Zelki!" My father calls to me. I turn, directing the flame at the rock wall beside me just in the nick of time. I am ashamed. He has warned me.

Tythos he will deal with later. He yells at him to leave, and my brother slinks away, muttering apologies, shaken. My father tells me to walk with him. He counsels me, reminds me the importance of control. He tells me I am strong, that I will be the largest of my brothers, a great warrior, but I must learn control. "I may not always be here to save you from yourself," he says.

"Yes, you will," I tell him with a ready grin. "You are a great Drako-ryan. You are a mighty dragon. You will be an ancient..."

The image dissolves and time accelerates now. They are happy images. Lessons and feasts and celebrations. I am flying again. I look to my left and see a flash of my golden wing. I am Imryth. I am flying with my father. We communicate without words. I am telling him I do not want to burn the fields. I do not understand why we must.

He tells me man will never accept our dragon side, that man is too flawed to be allowed back in power. He tells me we must manage them, just as they manage the crops and livestock we allow them to breed. We protect them. When winters are hard, we supply them with food, keep the wolves away. But they give us tribute – food we allow them to grow, and only on land we allow them to use. The rest is burnt.

He tells me to dive. In my dragon sight, I see women rushing to grab their children. They have seen our passing shadows through the clouds, and they are screaming. I do not want to do this, but I do it anyway. I target a rolling field just bursting with green. It takes only seconds to turn it black.

I ask my father about our servants. He tells me they are a different kind of man, the kind found under the earth, stouter and simpler and more loyal. But the other men – those who till the land – they are different. Left alone to unite, they would choose a king to rally under, to fight. We cannot let that happen. We keep them dependent. All we require is tribute. Food. And once a year, a daughter.

"Why can we not just deal with them in our man form?" I ask.

"Because," he responds, "you do not deal with your foe in your weakest form."

More years fly by. Flashes of memory. Sparring matches, training. We follow father into the army. Although we have known centuries of peace, we must always be ready. Readiness makes for peace, our father says.

And then a dark cloud envelops me. I feel a chill. The old man's face from under the hood. "Danger," he says. "We are not alone. The witches have seen a portent."

I feel heat in my face. Everything is dark. I am afraid. I hear screams. I am flying over a field. There are pools of blood, wounded dragons turning from brilliant colors to dull gray as they die. One falls from the sky, hitting the earth with a thud. I hear flapping. I do not want to turn. I see a dragon, larger and fiercer than any of us. It zooms past, laying down a swath of flame.

War. Our castle is under siege. What do the dragons want? I ask the Oracle as I land and fold my blue wings. "Why do they attack us? Who are they?"

ShadowFell, Olin the Wise says. The witches have warned us, he says. These are dark dragons, different. They are trying to get to the Mystic Mountain. What they want is there. We cannot let them have it. They want magic.

All the knights of the empire rally to the base of the mountain. It is hazy here. I do not see. I only feel. Heat and pain and loss but also bravery and determination. I see a massive orange dragon rise from a subterranean cave. It is Vukurcis, King of the Drakoryan Empire. He is swathed in a circle of blue flame – a magical fire shield conjured by the witches, the Wyrd. He fights the largest black dragon as we, his soldiers, battle the enemy in the sky and on the field.

My father fights by my side, incinerating a ShadowFell rocketing towards us.

Then, through the smoke, I see it. The king's magical shield is beginning to fade.

"Father," I say, but he has seen it, too, and flies to the king's side. King Vukurcis is in danger. The peak is crumbling beneath him and the ShadowFell King. King Vukurcis is close to falling when my father flies headlong into the side of the enemy dragon. He knocks it backwards, but as the ShadowFell falls, the hooked claw on the wing joint catches my father's chest, opening it. He falls from the other side. The enemy dragon recovers before hitting the ground, but upon seeing so many of his soldiers slain, roars in defeat and retreats.

I do not want to see the next vision. I feel the pain before the image comes into view. I am seeing now through the eyes of all my mates. Our father, Rymoth, is lying on a rock. A large man in a crown holds our father's hand. It is King Vukurcis returned to his Drakoryan form. Olin the Wise kneels by his side, a hand on my father's head.

"Can he be saved?" asks the king.

"There is nothing that can be done," the Oracle says.

"Our pools!" Zelki is demanding, but Olin shakes his head.

"The pools of the Wyrd," Tythos looks at the Oracle, but our father, his face ashen under the lowering cloak of death, shakes his head.

"I wanted the same for your mother, but in her wisdom, she forbid it. I have lived my life, but it is time to go. Now, I will live on through you, my sons." Final words fall from his lips. "Hold fast your bonds."

I can't breathe for sobbing from the collective pain. I am drifting now, moving through channels of time. The tide of life moves on. There is a land to rule, responsibilities to be met. My mates live with their grief, weaving the loss of their father and mother into the rich tapestry of their lives. They are in full manhood now. They are anxious. All grows dark.

I look at them from above now, hovering. It is a different perspective, detached, as I watch them fight. They fight as dragons, bloodying one another. I feel their pain even as I observe as an outsider. There is rage and a sense of competitive drive that is fierce and primal. Zelki defeats Imryth. Zelki defeats Tythos. Drorgros defeats Zelki.

And then, it grows dark for the last time. I am a dragon. I am flying. I am Drorgros the Dragon. The sun glints off my green wings. I am speeding through the clouds. I see something in the distance. A cliff. A ledge. There is a woman, small and blonde and afraid. I dive, dropping straight down, then curve up, pumping my wings as I rise. I look her in the eye. She stares back. I land on the ledge, set fire to her bonds. I know her. Somehow, I know her. She looks into my eye. She is not afraid. I feel myself smile. I cannot help it, but the human gesture on the visage of a dragon terrifies her. She screams. I pluck her from the cliff...

I hear myself gasp, like a drowning person come up through the water.

"Breathe...breathe...that's it." My mates are encouraging me to take in the air that I need. It is a struggle. "Come on. You can do it." "That's it, my beauty." "You've done it."

Their voices are so clear, but as I adjust my eyes to current surroundings, I understand that they are not speaking to me. I am hearing their thoughts.

"I saw what you saw. Felt what you felt," I say without words.

"Yes, you did. And you always will," they answer with their minds.

They wrap their arms around me, holding me in their circle, my Drakoryan mates, men who become dragons through a magic I am determined to understand, but inside as soft and human as the mate they have vowed to protect.

I am theirs. And they are mine.

***

"The Deepening is like losing your virginity all over again." Enid hands me a cup of sweet wine as she seeks to explain what I've been through.

"That is a good comparison," says an olive-skinned woman who was introduced to me as Daka. "Only it is not just you who is laid bare and exposed. Your mates share in your vulnerability. Lord Enrik says a Drakoryan, even if told what to expect, is as affected by the Deepening as his mate."

The other women nod.

We are sitting by a pool in the Crystal Cavern. The other Drakoryans will leave tomorrow, but tonight is for us women. They were waiting for me here, after the Deepening, and gently embraced me when I walked in, spent and still a little disoriented.

They are warm and strong, these women who share in my fate. All were seized by dragons, some from my village, some from other villages I have never heard of. They each have their own stories. They will share them. They say we have time, and from them I learn other secrets. I learn that the Deepening grants more than a bond. When a Drakoryan deepens with a mate, he gifts her with some of his life force, giving her exceptionally good health and a supernaturally long lifespan. Human women can still die – of injury, illness, in childbirth – but it is rare.

My induction into the world grants me membership into a special sisterhood. Enid is the one who gives me the necklace that all the women wear – a gift, she tells me, from the witches.

"The Wyrd send a message through us," she says as she fastens it around my neck. "You are now one of us, Lyla. You are now a Fire Bride."

I lift the pendant. It looks like frosted glass, but inside is a tiny, living flame. It changes color as it burns – green, blue, red, gold. I nearly cry with joy.

I still have questions. They laugh when I say this. You will always have questions, they say. But you will learn.

"Knowledge is not hidden here." A small, beautiful woman with a tight cap of red curls moves to sit beside me. "I expected my mates would lock me away and breed me to death. I was angry. I fought them. But no Drakoryan is matched with a mate he cannot handle. I challenge mine, but they need someone who keeps life interesting."

"Not mine," says Enid, smoothing my hair over my shoulder. "Mine prefer predictability. They take too much to heart. I am their haven, their comfort."

"What will I be?" I ask.

Enid smiles. "That will be up to you, Lyla. What do you want to be?"

I know what I want to be. I want to be happy. I know I love my Drakoryan mates. I do not want to be without them. But I also know that I will never be truly content until I can get word to my mother and my aunt that I survived. I do not want to defy my mates, but I'm committed to bringing peace to my mother, to easing her pain.

But for now, I will establish myself here. I will accept my fate, even as I forge my own path in this wild and mysterious world.

I was, after all, raised to be strong. I am a loved daughter, the niece of a priestess. I am Lyla, bonded mate to the Lords of Fra'hir. I am a Fire Bride.

My story is just beginning.

A PREVIEW OF BOOK TWO: FIRE BRIDE

Prologue

Once upon a time there was a king who had everything a king could ever want.

He had riches, a powerful army, and a fine castle with a high parapet overlooking all the lands he ruled.

He was King Eknor, and after years of making war, he was finally able to bask in his victories. He had defeated the kings of the valley. He had defeated the kings of the highlands. He had defeated all the kings in between. He had stormed their castles, overpowering them with such overwhelming force that most surrendered right away. Of those who had not, all that remained were their severed heads, rotting on pikes.

Each morning the king would walk to the parapet and watch the sun rise and spread its golden glow over the lands he'd conquered. Day after day he did this, but one morning he realized his pride was beginning to ebb, like the slow leak of air from a punctured lung.

Despite what he saw, he knew there was more land for the taking, land he could not see even from the tallest room of his castle.

King Eknor wondered what lay beyond the horizon, over the curve of the world. He imagined greater riches than he had in his storehouse, finer and bigger stags than those in his forest, mines filled with jewels and precious metals yet to be discovered.

Day after day he stared at the horizon. Day after day he became more restless, less content. The king knew not be satisfied until he had more. He knew he would not be satisfied until he traveled to where the world curved, to conquer what was yet unseen.

The queen urged caution. She urged contentment. Had he not conquered the other kings? Wasn't it enough? What lay beyond the curve of the world was not for him, she reasoned. She begged her husband to heed his Oracle, who'd warned that beyond the curve of the world lay the Wyld, its thick forests inhabited by beasts and fairie folk. The Wyld was full of magic, deep and old and unsullied by Man.

"Stay," the queen begged. "Rule your kingdom. Keep the peace."

But King Eknor would not be influenced by a mere woman, for what did women know of ambition? He ignored the queen's pleas. He told her would take their three sons— Arok, Dax, and Yrn. He would take half the army. The other half would stay behind to keep the peace. He would journey over the curve of the world, and conquer lands he could not see.

The queen wept, falling to her knees. She pressed her face into the king's gauntlet, pleading, but he pushed her to the throne room floor. As she lay there, sobbing her grief, the king walked away, followed by sons who had become as cold and ambitious as their father.

And they left. They traveled through the conquered lands, and over the curve of the world until they came to the edge of a wild, wild forest.

At its entrance stood a mighty stag, blocking the only way in, its antlers as broad as a spreading tree, its eyes fierce and protective.

"I am the guardian of this place," it said. "This is a land of magic. You are not welcome here." Some of the soldiers were afraid to hear a talking beast. They wanted to flee. But the king forbid it.

"I am King of Men," he snarled, "And your magic is no match for me."

King Eknor ordered his soldiers to kill the stag. They surrounded the creature, hemming it in. The stag tried to rush through the ring of horsemen, but could not. On the king's command, the soldiers fired upon the noble creature. It took many arrows, and when it finally fell, the king dismounted, drew his sword and approached the bloodied beast. The stag looked up through weary eyes and begged for its life. But the king refused, cutting its throat.

"Should we butcher it for meat, sire?" a soldier asked.

The king regarded the dead stag. "No need. The wood is full of beasts. Why haul our meat when we can kill another deer closer to where we break camp? Leave it to rot. We'll take the head for a trophy on the way back."

They continued through the wood.

At dusk, they made camp in a glen. The soldiers chopped down a gnarled yew, which groaned with each blow of the axe. They burned it for fire. The eldest prince shot a doe that came to the stream to drink, sending her orphaned fawn bleating into a thicket. He and his brothers set snares in the night, and in the morning found a russet fox, its paw caught in the loop. When it looked at the middle prince with hopeful eyes, he and his younger brother clubbed it to death and cast lots for its skin.

The carrion birds, realizing that Men meant Death, began following them, feeding on the creatures they needlessly felled. The princes' swords *and skinning knives stayed red with blood. They killed for fun, boasting of the fine trophies they would take once they had conquered whatever sovereign ruled this land, for despite what the Oracle told them, there was always a ruler, always a king. There was always someone to defeat.*

And they were right. There was a ruler of this realm, and it was angered by each senseless slaughter, each felled tree. The cries of the carrion birds, the coppery smell of blood and smoke, were an offense to this sovereign, who was more powerful than the king could imagine.

And unlike mortal men, the rulers of the Wyld had no need of bows and blades. Its weapons were in nature itself. It sent driving snow so thick that the king, the princes, and the soldiers lost their way in the wood. It sent knives of icy wind that pierced furs and armor and woolens beneath them. The men shook with cold. Their lips cracked and bled. Frost clung to their lashes and beards. Some begged to turn back.

But the king pressed on, refusing to admit defeat even when first horses, then soldiers, began to die from hunger. With each loss, he fancied he could hear laughter on the wind, and this enraged him. He rallied his dying men, not realizing he was leading them in endless circles.

When his own horse fell beneath him, he demanded the mount of his most loyal knight, leaving man stranded, for no horse could carry two by this point.

It was only when he and his sons – the sole survivors – were killing their last horse for food – that King Eknor realized the folly of his pride. He'd betrayed his best knights. He'd lost half his army.

"What have I done?" he thought, and with that one question, the weather calmed.

The king and his sons, on foot now and weak, discovered path that led from the forest to a cave. They entered, leaning against one another for support. They needed shelter. They needed warmth. They were tired of eating snow. They needed water. They could hear it dripping, and stumbled through the dark passages, following the sound.

When the cave opened to the cavern, what they saw made them cry for joy. It was a pool, the surface smooth and glassy. The king stumbled towards it, beckoning his sons to follow. But their legs gave way before they could reach it, and they lay on the stone floor, helpless.

The king looked up then to see a woman sitting on a stone by the pool. How had he missed her before?

He reached up and beckoned her to him. "Woman," he called, "my sons and I are dying. Bring us water."

The woman did not move. She just stayed where she was, on the rock.

"These are no ordinary waters you ask for," she said. "They are healing waters."

"More's the better," he replied. I am no ordinary man. I am King Eknor. And you will bring me and my sons drink."

"A king you say?" She smiled but did not move

The king lifted his head. Was she mocking him? Why wasn't she obeying? He gritted his teeth in fury and tried to crawl forward, but his legs were as lead. Beside him, his sons groaned with thirst and pain.

"Bring me water!" His command echoed off the walls of the cave. "I demand it! Bring me water or…"

"Or what?" The woman stood. She was clad in blue and had long silver hair. She walked over and knelt beside him. "What will you do if I refuse to obey, great king of men? Will you shoot me full of arrows? Hack me apart with an axe and burn my body? Catch me in a snare and strip me of my skin?" She reached out a warm hand and cupped his chin. "You may have been a king once, but no longer. Now you are but a beggar."

And King Eknor was afraid, for he realized she was right. He could not move. His life was ebbing away. His three sons, lying beside him, were barely breathing.

"Would you like to know how long you wandered in my forest?" she asked.

"I know how long I wandered." He licked his dry lips, looking longingly at the pool. "Days and days."

She shook her head. "No. It was years. Years and years. Time moves differently here. "Would you like to know what has happened to your kingdom while you've been away?"

The king felt a chill run through him, a chill deeper than any he'd felt in the forest. He was afraid now. He did not want to know. She told him anyway.

"When you didn't return, those you conquered banded together to wage war. They defeated what remained of your army. They sacked your castle. One of them took your wife. He was a kinder man. She loved him, and bore him children." She paused. "But that was a hundred years ago."

"You lie," he said through gritted teeth, but she moved her fingers to his temple, and he saw all she'd told him flash through his mind, and knew it was true. His cries filled the cave.

"All this?" he sobbed, spittle running from his mouth. "Because I felled a tree, killed a beast?"

"Did you?" She stood and turned, looking across the pool. From the shadows the stag emerged.

"My consort," she said. She curtseyed to the stag. "My lord."

The stag bowed in return. Its voice was the deep voice of the earth, the sound of wind and water. "My lady."

The woman turned back to the king.

"We are two parts of whole. We are Lord and Lady. God and Goddess. Duality. It is how the Wyld keeps its balance. You have a duality, too, I think. You are a man, but also a terrible monster. As punishment for what you've done, you will die, King Eknor. And your line will be cursed forever more with the task of balancing these beasts.

She lifted her hands. "Come," she commanded, and the three princes rose, not by their own will, but as in a trance. Like puppets dancing on invisible strings, they lurched past their father to the pool. There, they knelt like dogs and drank.

"Behold," the lady said, and the princes began to shiver and then to scream.

"Father!" they cried. "Father!" But the king could not aid them. He could only watch as his sons burst into flames of different colors – one fire white, one sunset orange, one purple – that shot to the ceiling. Then the flames began to shrink and reform into something solid, and there, where his sons had stood, were three small winged beasts.

The lady reached down to pet them one by one. "See what you put inside your sons? The dragon is the greediest of creatures. A dragon is never satisfied. Its appetite can be controlled only with the strongest will. I have used the old magic to draw out what you put inside them, to make it manifest. From this day forth, your sons will not be fully human, but a new race – half drake, half man. They will possess the fullness of their terrible dragon might, but their human side will grieve over how this destruction further removes them from all they love. They will war with man and dragon alike, never accepted by either, but dependent on what they deign to be the weakest – human females — for only through human woman can their line continue."

King Eknor understood now. The God and Goddess had tested him. He had failed. This was the awful price. He used the last of his strength to plead then, to plead for mercy he knew he did not deserve.

"*My lady. My lord...*" Tears coursed down the king's cheeks as he looked towards his sons who were hissing and backing away, all recognition of him gone from their yellow eyes. "*Let them...be redeemed. If you've any mercy, grant them the capacity to find peace, to make it.*"

The Goddess looked up at the God, who glanced the three juvenile dragon. He considered them dispassionately before giving a barely perceptible nod. The lady had a merciful side, and her consort could not deny her.

The lady knelt again, took the king's face in her hands and fixed him with eyes of kindness.

"*I will fulfill your dying wish,*" she told him. "*I will grant the Drakoryan the will to learn, although the path will be very long, and very hard. I will grant them protection through my priestesses, the Wyrd. In time, they will become a great and mighty race, so long as they keep the balance their father could not.*"

The king nodded. "*I am tired,*" he said. "*So tired.*"

"*Then take your ease,*" she said, cradling his head in her lap.

And there, in the cave, the king closed his eyes for the last time.

About The Author

USA Today bestselling author Ava Sinclair has been writing erotic romance since the late 1990's, capitalizing on the spicy readers' desire for kink long before Fifty Shades of Grey brought it mainstream.

She's written over fifty books and is enjoys weaving conflict and relatable situations into her books.

She lives on a farm in the foothill country of Virginia. When she's not writing, she's fussing over her cats or tending to her dairy goats and Shetland sheep.

Connect with Ava

Let's be friends. Hey, it's possible today thanks to social media. Here's where you can find me.

On Facebook I have a main page, an author's page – both under the name Ava Sinclair - and a private group – Ava's Risque Reading Room.

I'm also on Instagram and TikTok as **@authoringava**

Other Books in the Drakoryan Bride Series

Milton Keynes UK
Ingram Content Group UK Ltd.
UKHW022343020823
426203UK00017B/748

9 798223 364955